'Luca, what are you doing?'

But the defensive tartness was gone out of Serena's voice.

He pulled her in closer. The darkness wrapped around them but failed to hide that bright blue gaze or the gold of her hair. The slant of her stunning cheekbones.

She wasn't pulling away.

Luca's body was on fire. From somewhere he found his voice and it sounded coarse, rough. 'What am I doing?'

This...

And then he pulled her right into him and his mouth found hers with unerring precision. Her breasts swelled against his chest—in outrage? He didn't know, because he was falling over the very thin edge of his control.

When he felt her resistance give way after an infinitesimal moment triumph surged through his body. He couldn't think any more because he was swept up in the decadent darkness of a kiss that intoxicated him and reminded him of only one other similar moment...with her... seven years before.

BILLIONAIRE BROTHERS

*One raised in luxury in Brazil,
the other on the streets of Italy...*

Luca Fonseca lives with the shame of his father's
unethical dealings and his own mistake of falling for
a beautiful face. Now this cold-hearted Brazilian is
determined to restore his family's reputation—
with or without his twin brother's help.

Embittered Max Fonseca Roselli
has shunned his heritage and his brother, and despite
raising himself on the streets of Rome has carved out
his own successful life. He, too, wants respectability—
but he has a very different plan...

*Two women will bring these brothers together—
but is it enough to restore their brotherly bond?*

Find out in:
FONSECA'S FURY
January 2015

Don't miss Max's story in:
THE BRIDE FONSECA NEEDS
June 2015

FONSECA'S FURY

BY
ABBY GREEN

Abby Green spent her teens reading Mills & Boon® romances. She then spent many years working in the film and TV industry as an assistant director. One day, while standing outside an actor's trailer in the rain, she thought: *There has to be more than this.* So she sent off a partial manuscript to Mills & Boon. After many rewrites they accepted her first book and an author was born.

She lives in Dublin, Ireland, and you can find out more here: www.abby-green.com

Recent titles by the same author:

WHEN DA SILVA BREAKS THE RULES
  (Blood Brothers)
WHEN CHRISTAKOS MEETS HIS MATCH
  (Blood Brothers)
WHEN FALCONE'S WORLD STOPS TURNING
  (Blood Brothers)
FORGIVEN BUT NOT FORGOTTEN?

Did you know these are also available as eBooks?
Visit www.millsandboon.co.uk

This is for Helen Kane—
thanks for going to Dubai and letting me rent out your
house and possibly the most idyllic office space in
Dublin. And I do forgive you for leaving me behind in
Kathmandu (on my birthday!) while you went off and
romanced your own Mills and Boon hero! x

CHAPTER ONE

SERENA DEPIERO SAT in the plush ante-room and looked at the name on the opposite wall, spelled out in matt chrome lettering, and reeled.

Roseca Industries and Philanthropic Foundation.

Renewed horror spread through her. It had only been on the plane to Rio de Janeiro, when she'd been reading the extra information on the charity given to her by her boss, that she'd become aware that it was part of a much bigger organisation. An organisation run and set up by Luca Fonseca. The name Roseca was apparently an amalgamation of his father and mother's surnames. And Serena wasn't operating on a pay grade level high enough to require her to be aware of this knowledge before now.

Except here she was, outside the CEO's office, waiting to be called in to see the one man on the planet who had every reason to hate her guts. Why hadn't he sacked her months ago, as soon as she'd started working for him? Surely he must have known? An insidious suspicion took root: perhaps he'd orchestrated this all along, to lull her into a false sense of security before letting her crash spectacularly to the ground.

That would be breathtakingly cruel, and yet this man

owed her nothing but his disdain. She owed *him*. Serena knew that there was a good chance her career in fund-raising was about to be over before it had even taken off. And at that thought she felt a spurt of panic mixed with determination. Surely enough time had passed now? Surely, even if this *was* some elaborate revenge cooked up by Luca Fonseca as soon as he'd known she was working for him, she could try to convince him how sorry she was?

But before she could wrap her head around it any further a door opened to her right and a sleek dark-haired woman dressed in a grey suit emerged.

'Senhor Fonseca will see you now, Miss DePiero.'

Serena's hands clenched tightly around her handbag. She felt like blurting out, *But I don't want to see him!*

But she couldn't. As much as she couldn't just flee. The car that had met her at the airport to deliver her here still had her luggage in its boot.

As she stood up reluctantly a memory assailed her with such force it almost knocked her sideways: Luca Fonseca in a bloodstained shirt, with a black eye and a split lip. Dark stubble shadowing his swollen jaw. He'd been behind the bars of a jail cell, leaning against a wall, brooding and dangerous. But then he'd looked up and narrowed that intensely dark blue gaze on her, and an expression of icy loathing had come over his face.

He'd straightened and moved to the bars, wrapping his fingers around them almost as if he was imagining they were her neck. Serena had stopped dead at the battered sight of him. He'd spat out, *'Damn you, Serena DePiero, I wish I'd never laid eyes on you.'*

'Miss DePiero? Senhor Fonseca is waiting.'

The clipped and accented voice shattered Serena's

memory and she forced her feet to move, taking her past the unsmiling woman and into the palatial office beyond.

She hated that her heart was thumping so hard when she heard the door snick softly shut behind her. For the first few seconds she saw no one, because the entire back wall of the office was a massive window and it framed the most amazingly panoramic view of a city Serena had ever seen.

The Atlantic glinted dark blue in the distance, and inland from that were the two most iconic shapes of Rio de Janeiro: the Sugar Loaf and Christ the Redeemer high on Corcovado. In between were countless other tall buildings, right up to the coast. To say that the view was breathtaking was an understatement.

And then suddenly it was eclipsed by the man who moved into her line of vision. Luca Fonseca. For a second past and present merged and Serena was back in that nightclub, seeing him for the first time.

He'd stood so tall and broad against the backdrop of that dark and opulent place. Still. She'd never seen anyone so still, yet with such a commanding presence. People had skirted around him. Men suspicious, envious. Women lustful.

In a dark suit and open-necked shirt he'd been dressed much the same as other men, but he'd stood out from them all by dint of that sheer preternatural stillness and the incredible forcefield of charismatic magnetism that had drawn her to him before she could stop herself.

Serena blinked. The dark and decadent club faded. She couldn't breathe. The room was instantly stifling. Luca Fonseca looked different. It took her sluggish brain a second to function enough for her to realise that he looked different because his hair was longer, slightly unruly. And he had a dark beard that hugged his jaw. It made him look even more intensely masculine.

He was wearing a light-coloured open-necked shirt tucked into dark trousers. For all the world the urbane, civilised businessman in his domain, and yet the vibe coming from him was anything but civilised.

He crossed his arms over that massive chest and then he spoke. 'What the hell do you think you're doing here, DePiero?'

Serena moved further into the vast office, even though it was in the opposite direction from where she wanted to go. She couldn't take her eyes off him even if she wanted to.

She forced herself to speak, to act as if seeing him again wasn't as shattering as it was. 'I'm here to start working in the fundraising department for the global communities charity.'

'Not any more, you're not,' Fonseca said tersely.

Serena flushed. 'I didn't know you were…involved until I was on my way over here.'

Fonseca made a small sound like a snort. 'An unlikely tale.'

'It's true,' Serena blurted out. 'I had no idea the charity was linked to the Roseca Foundation. Believe me, if I'd had any idea I wouldn't have agreed to come here.'

Luca Fonseca moved around the table and Serena's eyes widened. For a big man, he moved with innate grace, and that incredible quality of self-containment oozed from every pore. It was intensely captivating.

He admitted with clear irritation, 'I wasn't aware that you were working in the Athens office. I don't micromanage my smaller charities abroad because I hire the best staff to do that for me—although I'm reconsidering my policy after this. If I'd known they'd hired you, of all people, you would have been let go long before now.'

His mouth twisted with recrimination.

'But I have to admit that I was intrigued enough to have you brought here instead of just leaving you at the airport until we could put you on a return flight.'

So he hadn't even known she was working for him. Serena's hands curled into fists at her sides. His dismissive arrogance set her nerves even more on edge.

He glanced at a big platinum watch on his wrist. 'I have a spare fifteen minutes before you are to be delivered back to the airport.'

Like an unwanted package. He was firing her.

He hitched a hip onto the corner of his desk, for all the world as if they were having a normal conversation amidst the waves of tension. 'Well, DePiero? What the hell is Europe's most debauched ex-socialite doing working for minimum wage in a small charity office in Athens?'

Only hours ago Serena had been buoyant at the thought of her new job. A chance to prove to her somewhat over-protective family that she was going to be fine. She'd been ecstatic at the thought of her independence. And now this man was going to ensure that everything she'd fought so hard for was for naught.

For years she had been the *enfant terrible* of the Italian party scene, frequently photographed, with reams of newsprint devoted to her numerous exploits which had been invariably blown out of proportion. Nevertheless, Serena knew well that there was enough truth behind the headlines to make her feel that ever-present prick of shame.

'Look,' she said, hating the way her voice had got husky with repressed emotion and shock at facing this blast from her past, 'I know you must hate me.'

Luca Fonseca smiled. But his expression was hard. 'Hate? Don't flatter yourself, DePiero, *hate* is a very inadequate description of my feelings where you are concerned.'

Another poisonous memory assailed her: a battered Luca, handcuffed by Italian police, being dragged bodily to an already loaded-up van, snarling, *'You set me up, you bitch!'* at Serena, who had been moments away from being handed into a police car herself, albeit minus the handcuffs.

They'd insisted on everyone being hauled in to the police station. He'd tried to jerk free of the burly police officers and that had earned him a thump to his belly, making him double over. Serena had been stupefied. Transfixed with shock.

He'd rasped out painfully, just before disappearing into the police van, 'She planted the drugs on *me* to save herself.'

Serena tried to force the memories out of her head. 'Mr Fonseca, I didn't plant those drugs in your pockets... I don't know who did, but it wasn't me. I tried to contact you afterwards...but you'd left Italy.'

He made a sound of disgust. 'Afterwards? You mean after you'd returned from your shopping spree in Paris? I saw the pictures. Avoiding being prosecuted for possession of drugs and continuing your hedonistic existence was all in a week's work for you, wasn't it?'

Serena couldn't avoid the truth; no matter how innocent she was, this man *had* suffered because of their brief association. The lurid headlines were still clear in her mind: *DePiero's newest love interest? Brazilian billionaire Fonseca caught with drugs after raid on Florence's most exclusive nightclub, Den of Eden.*

But before Serena could defend herself Luca was standing up and walking closer, making her acutely aware of his height and powerful frame. Her mouth dried.

When he was close enough that she could make out the dark chest hair curling near the open V of his shirt, he sent an icy look from her face to her feet, and then said derisively, 'A far cry from that lame excuse for a dress.'

Serena could feel heat rising at the reminder of how she'd been dressed that night. How she'd dressed most nights. She tried again, even though it was apparent that her attempt to defend herself had fallen on deaf ears. 'I really didn't have anything to do with those drugs. I promise. It was all a huge misunderstanding.'

He looked at her for a long moment, clearly incredulous, before tipping his head back and laughing so abruptly that Serena flinched.

When his eyes met hers again they still sparkled with cold mirth, and that sensual mouth was curved in an equally cold smile.

'I have to hand it to you—you've got some balls to come in here and protest your innocence after all this time.'

Serena's nails scored her palms, but she didn't notice. 'It's true. I know what you must think…'

She stopped, and had to push down the insidious

reminder that it was what *everyone* had thought. Erroneously.

'I didn't do those kinds of drugs.'

Any hint of mirth, cold or otherwise, vanished from Luca Fonseca's visage. 'Enough with protesting your innocence. You had Class A drugs in that pretty purse and you conveniently slipped them into my pocket as soon as it became apparent that the club was being raided.'

Feeling sick now, Serena said, 'It must have been someone else in the crush and panic.'

Fonseca moved even closer to Serena then, and she gulped and looked up. She felt hot, clammy.

His voice was low, seductive. 'Do I need to remind you of how close we were that night, Serena? How easy it must have been for you to divest yourself of incriminating evidence?'

Serena could recall all too clearly that his arms had been like steel bands around her, with hers twined around his neck. Her mouth had been sensitive and swollen, her breathing rapid. Someone had rushed over to them on the dance floor—some acquaintance of Serena's who had hissed, *'There's a raid.'*

And Luca Fonseca thought… He thought that during those few seconds before chaos had struck she'd had the presence of mind to somehow slip drugs onto his person?

He said now, 'I'm sure it was a move you'd perfected over the years, which was why I felt nothing.'

He stepped back and Serena could take a breath again. But then he walked around her, and her skin prickled. She was acutely aware of his regard and wanted to adjust her suit, which felt constrictive.

She closed her eyes and then opened them again,

turning around to face him. 'Mr Fonseca, I'm just looking for a chance—'

He held up his hand and Serena stopped. His expression was worse than cold now: it was completely indecipherable.

He clicked his fingers, as if something just occurred to him, and his lip curled. 'Of *course*—it's your family, isn't it? They've clipped your wings. Andreas Xenakis and Rocco De Marco would never tolerate a return to your debauched ways, and you're still *persona non grata* in the social circles who fêted you before. You and your sister certainly landed on your feet, in spite of your father's fall from grace.'

Disgust was etched on his hard features.

'Lorenzo DePiero will never be able to show his face again after the things he did.'

Serena felt nauseous. She of all people didn't need to be reminded of her father's corruption and many crimes.

But Luca wasn't finished. 'I think you're doing this under some sort of sufferance, to prove to your new-found family that you've changed... In return for what? An allowance? A palatial home back in Italy, your old stomping ground? Or perhaps you'll stay in Athens, where the stench of your tarnished reputation is a little less...pungent? After all, it's where you'll have the protection of your younger sister who, if I recall correctly, was the one who regularly cleaned up your messes.'

Fire raced up Serena's spine at hearing him mention her family—and especially her sister. A sense of protectiveness overwhelmed her. They were everything to her and she would never, ever let them down. They had saved her. Something this cold, judgmental man would never understand.

Serena was jet-lagged, gritty-eyed, and in shock at seeing this man again, and it was evident in her voice now, as she lashed back heatedly, 'My family have nothing to do with this. And nothing to do with *you*.'

Luca Fonseca looked at Serena incredulously. 'I'm sure your family have everything to do with this. Did you drop a tantalising promise of generous donations from them in return for a move up the career ladder?'

Serena flushed and got out a strangled-sounding, 'No, of course not.'

But the way she avoided his eyes told Luca otherwise. She wouldn't have had to drop anything but the most subtle of hints. The patronage of either her half-brother, Rocco De Marco, or her brother-in-law, Andreas Xenakis, could secure a charity's fortunes for years to come. And, as wealthy as he was in his own right, the foundation would always need to raise money. Disgusted that his own staff might have been so easily manipulated, and suddenly aware of how heated his blood was, Luca stepped back.

He was grim. 'I am not going to be a convenient conduit through which you try to fool everyone into thinking you've changed.'

Serena just looked at him, and he saw her long, graceful throat work, as if she couldn't quite get out what she wanted to say. He felt no pity for her.

She couldn't be more removed from the woman of his memory of seven years ago, when she'd been golden and sinuous and provocative. The woman in front of him now looked pale, and as if she was going for an interview in an insurance office. Her abundantly sexy white-blonde hair had been tamed into a staid chignon. And yet even that, and the sober dark suit, couldn't dim her incredible natural beauty or those piercing bright blue eyes.

Those eyes had hit him right in the solar plexus as soon as she'd walked into his office, when he'd been able to watch her unobserved for a few seconds. And the straight trousers couldn't hide those famously long legs. The generous swell of her breasts pushed against the silk of her shirt.

Disgust curled through him to notice her like this. Had he learnt nothing? She should be prostrating herself at his feet in abject apology for turning his life upside down, but instead she had the temerity to defend herself: *'My family have nothing to do with this.'*

His clear-headed focus was being eroded in this woman's presence. Why was he even wondering anything about her? He didn't care what her nefarious motivations were. He'd satisfied whatever curiosity he'd had.

He clenched his jaw. 'Your time is up. The car will be waiting outside for your return to the airport. And I do sincerely hope to never lay eyes on you again.'

So why was it so hard to rip his gaze *off* her?

Anger and self-recrimination coursed through Luca as he stepped around Serena and stalked back to his desk, expecting to hear the door open and close.

When he didn't, he spun round and spat out tersely, 'We have nothing more to discuss.'

The fact that she had gone paler was something that Luca didn't like to acknowledge that he'd noticed. Or his very bizarre dart of concern. No woman evoked concern in him. He could see her swallow again, that long, graceful throat moving, and then her soft, husky voice, with that slightest hint of an Italian accent, crossed the space between them.

'I'm just asking for a chance. Please.'

Luca's mouth opened and closed. He was stunned. Once he declared what he wanted no one questioned him. Until now. And this woman, of all people? Serena DePiero had a less than zero chance of Luca reconsidering his decision. The fact that she was still in his office set his nerves sizzling just under his skin. Irritating him.

But instead of admitting defeat and turning round, the woman stepped closer. Further away from the door.

Luca had an urge to snarl and stalk over to her, to put her over his shoulder, physically remove her from his presence. But right then, with perfect timing, the memory of her lush body pressed against his, her soft mouth yielding to his forceful kiss, exploded into his consciousness and within a nano-second he was battling a surge of blood to his groin.

Damn her. Witch.

She was at the other side of his desk. Blue eyes huge, her bearing as regal as a queen's, reminding him effortlessly of her impeccable lineage.

Her voice was low and she clasped her hands together in front of her, knuckles white. 'Mr Fonseca, I came here with the best of intentions to do work for your charity, despite what you may believe. I'll do anything to prove to you how committed I am.'

Anger surged at her persistence. At her meek *Mr Fonseca.*

Luca uncrossed his arms and placed his hands on the table in front of him, leaning forward. '*You* are the reason I had to rebuild my reputation and people's trust in my charitable work—not to mention trust in my family's mining consortium. I spent months, *years*, undoing the damage of that one night. Debauchery is all very well and good, as you must know, but the stigma of possessing Class A drugs does tend to last. The truth is that once those pictures of us together in the nightclub surfaced I *had* no defence.'

It almost killed Luca now to recall how he had instinctively shielded Serena from the police and detectives who had stormed the club, which was when she must have taken the opportunity to plant the drugs on him.

He thought of the paparazzi pictures of her shopping in Paris while he'd been leaving Italy under a cloud of disgrace, and bitterness laced his voice. 'Meanwhile you were oblivious to the fallout, continuing your hedonistic existence. And after all that, you have the temerity to think that I would so much as allow your name to be mentioned in the same sentence as mine?'

If possible, she paled even more, displaying the genes she'd inherited from her half-English mother, a classic English rose beauty.

He straightened up. 'You disgust me.'

Serena was dimly aware that on some level his words were hurting her in a place that she shouldn't be feeling hurt. But something dogged deep inside had pushed her to plead. And she had.

His eyes were like dark, hard sapphires. Impervious to heat or cold or her pleas. He was right. He was the one man on the planet who would never give her a chance. She was delusional to have thought even for a second that he might hear her out.

The atmosphere in the office was positively glacial in comparison to the gloriously sunny day outside. Luca Fonseca was just looking at her. Serena's belly sank. He wasn't even going to say another word. He'd said everything. He'd just wanted to see her, to torture her. Make her realise just how much he hated her—as if she had been in any doubt.

She finally admitted defeat and turned to the door. There would be no reprieve. Hitching up her chin in a tiny gesture of dignity, she didn't glance back at him, not wanting to see that arctic expression again. As if she was something distasteful on the end of his shoe.

She opened the door, closed it behind her, and was met by his cool assistant who was waiting for her. And who'd undoubtedly been privy to the plans of her boss well before Serena had been. Silently she was escorted downstairs.

Her humiliation was complete.

Ten minutes later Luca spoke tersely into his phone. 'Call me as soon as you know she's boarded and the plane has left.'

When he'd terminated the call Luca swivelled around in his high-backed chair to face the view. His blood was still boiling with a mixture of anger and arousal. Why had he indulged in the dubious desire to see her face to face again? All it had done was show him his own weakness for her.

He hadn't even known she was on her way to Rio until his assistant had informed him; the significance of her arrival had only come to light far too late to do anything about it.

Serena DePiero. Just her name brought an acrid taste of poison to his mouth. And yet the image that accompanied her name was anything but poisonous. It was provocative. It was his first image of her in that night-club in Florence.

He'd known who she was, of course. No one could have gone to Florence and *not* known who the DePiero sisters were—famed for their light-haired, blue-eyed aristocratic beauty and their vast family fortune that stretched back to medieval times. Serena had been the media's darling. Despite her debauched existence, no matter what she did, they'd lapped it up and bayed for more.

Her exploits had been legendary: high-profile weekends in Rome, leaving hotels trashed and staff incandescent with rage. Whirlwind private jet trips to the Middle East on the whim of an equally debauched sheikh who fancied a party with his Eurotrash friends. And always pictured in various states of inebriation and loucheness that had only seemed to heighten her dazzling appeal.

The night he'd seen her she'd been in the middle of the dance floor in what could only be described as an excuse for a dress. Strapless gold lamé, with tassels barely covering the top of her toned golden thighs. Long white-blonde hair tousled and falling down her back and over her shoulders, brushing the enticing swell of a voluptuous cleavage. Her peers had jostled around her, vying for her attention, desperately trying to emulate her golden exclusiveness.

With her arms in the air, swaying to the hedonistic beat of music played by some world-class DJ, she had symbolised the very font of youth and allure and beauty. The kind of beauty that made grown men fall to their knees in wonder. A siren's beauty, luring them to their doom.

Luca's mouth twisted. He'd proved to be no better than any other mortal man when she'd lured him to his doom. He took responsibility for being in that club—

of course he did. But from the moment she'd sashayed over to stand in front of him everything had grown a little hazy. And Luca was not a person who got hazy. No matter how stunning the woman. His whole life was about being clear and focused, because he had a lot to achieve.

But her huge bright blue eyes had seared him alive, igniting every nerve-ending, blasting aside any concerns. Her skin was flawless, her aquiline nose a testament to her breeding. Her mouth had fascinated him. Perfectly sculpted lips. Not too full, not too thin, effortlessly hinting at a dark and sexy sensuality.

She'd said coquettishly, 'It's rude to stare, you know.'

And instead of turning on his heel in disgust at her reputation and her arrogance, Luca had felt the blood flow through his body, hardening it, and he'd drawled softly, 'I'd have to be blind not to be dazzled. Join me for a drink?'

She'd tossed her head and for a second Luca had thought he glimpsed something curiously vulnerable and weary in those stunning blue eyes, but it had to have been a trick of the strobing lights, because then she'd purred, 'I'd love to.'

The wisps of memory faded from Luca's mind. He hated it that even now, just thinking of her, was having an effect on his body. Seven years had passed, and yet he felt as enflamed by anger and desire as he had that night. A bruising, humiliating mix.

He'd just left Serena DePiero in no doubt as to what he thought of her. She'd effectively been fired from her job. So why wasn't there a feeling of triumph rushing through him? Why was there an unsettling, prickling feeling of...unfinished business?

And why was there the tiniest grudging sliver of admiration for the way she had not backed down from him and the way that small chin had tipped up ever so slightly just before she'd left?

CHAPTER TWO

THE HOTEL WAS a few blocks back from Copacabana beach. To say that it was basic was an understatement, but it was clean—which was the main thing. And cheap—which was good, considering Serena was living off her meagre savings from the last year. She took off her travelling clothes, which were well creased by now, and stepped into the tiny shower, relishing the luke-warm spray.

Her belly clenched minutely when she imagined Luca's reaction to her *not* leaving Rio but she pushed it aside. She'd been standing in line for the check-in when her sister had phoned her. Too heartsore to admit that she was coming home so soon, and suddenly aware that Athens didn't even really feel like home, Serena had made a spur-of-the-moment decision to tell a white lie and pretend everything was okay.

And, even though she'd hated lying—to her sister, of all people—she didn't regret it now. She was still angry at Luca Fonseca's easy dismissal of her, the way he'd toyed with her before kicking her out of his office.

It had been enough to propel her out of the airport and back into the city. She scrubbed her scalp with un-necessary force, not liking how turbulent her emotions still were after meeting him again, and she certainly didn't like admitting that he'd roused her to a kind of anger she hadn't felt in a long time. Angry enough to rebel...when she'd thought she'd left all that behind her.

When she emerged from the bathroom she had a towel hitched around her body and another one on her head, and was feeling no less disgruntled. She almost jumped out of her skin when a loud, persistent knocking came on her door.

Scrambling around to find something to put on, Serena called out to whoever it was to wait a second as she pulled on some underwear and faded jeans and a T-shirt. The towel fell off her head so her long hair hung damply down her back and over her shoulders.

She opened the door and it was as if someone had punched her in the stomach. She couldn't draw breath because Luca Fonseca was standing there, eyes shooting sparks at her, looking angrier than she'd ever seen him.

'What the hell are you doing here, DePiero?' he snarled.

Serena answered faintly, 'You seem to be asking me that a lot lately.'

And then the fright he'd just given her faded and the anger she'd been harbouring swelled back. Her hand gripped the door.

'Actually, I might ask the same of you—what the hell are *you* doing *here*, Fonseca?' Something occurred to her. 'And how on earth did you even know where I was?'

His mouth was a tight line. 'I told Sancho, my driver, to wait at the airport and make sure you got on the flight.'

The extent of how badly he'd wanted her gone hit

her. Her hand gripped the door even tighter. 'This is a free country, Fonseca. I decided to stay and do a little sightseeing, and as I no longer work for you I really don't think you have any jurisdiction here.'

She went to close the door in his face but he easily stopped her and stepped into the room, closing the door behind him and forcing her to take a step back.

His arctic gaze took in her appearance with derision and Serena crossed her arms over her braless chest, self-conscious.

'Mr Fonseca—'

'Enough with the *Mr Fonseca*. Why are you still here, Serena?'

His use of her name made something swoop inside her. She crossed her arms tighter. It reminded her bizarrely of how it had felt to kiss him in the middle of that dance floor. Dark and hot and intoxicating. No other man's kiss or touch had ever made her feel like that. She'd pulled back from him in shock, as if his kiss had incinerated her, right through to where she was still whole. *Herself.*

'Well?'

The curt question jarred Serena back to the present and she hated it that she'd remembered that feeling of exposure.

'I want to see Rio de Janeiro before going home.' As if she would confide that she also wanted to delay revealing the extent of her failure to her family for as long as possible.

Luca snorted indelicately. 'Do you have *any* idea where you are? Were you planning on taking a stroll along the beach later?'

Serena gritted her jaw. 'I was, actually. I'd invite

you to join me, but I'm sure you have better things to be doing.'

His sheer animal magnetism was almost overwhelming in the small space. The beard and his longer hair only added to his intense masculinity. Her skin prickled with awareness. She could feel her nipples tighten and harden against the barrier of her thin T-shirt and hated the unique way this man affected her above any other.

Luca was snarling again. 'Do you realise that you're in one of the most dangerous parts of Rio? You're just minutes from one of the worst *favelas* in the city.'

Serena resisted the urge to point out that that should please him. 'But the beach is just blocks away.'

Now he was grim. 'Yes, and no one goes near this end of the beach at night unless they're out to score some drugs or looking to get mugged. It's one of the most dangerous places in the city after dark.'

He stepped closer and his eyes narrowed on her speculatively.

'But maybe that's it? You're looking for some recreational enhancement? Maybe your family have you under their watch and you're relishing some freedom? Have you even told them you've been fired?'

Serena's arms fell to her sides and she barely noticed Luca's gaze dropping to her chest before coming up again. All she felt was an incredible surge of anger and hatred for this man and his perspicacity—even if it wasn't entirely accurate.

Disgusted at the part of her that wanted to try and explain herself to him, she spat out, 'What's the point?'

She stalked around Luca and reached for the door handle, but before she could turn it and open the door an arm came over her head, keeping the door shut. She turned and folded her arms again, glaring up at Luca, conscious of her bare feet and damp hair, trying desperately not to let his sheer physicality affect her.

'If you don't leave in five seconds I'll start screaming.'

Luca kept his arm on the door, semi caging Serena in. 'The manager will just assume we're having fun. You can't be so naive that you didn't notice this place rents rooms by the hour.'

Serena felt hot. First of all at thinking of this man making her scream with pleasure and then at her own naivety.

'Of course I didn't,' she snapped, feeling vulnerable. She scooted out from under Luca's arm and put some space between them.

Luca crossed his arms. 'No, I can imagine you didn't. After all, it's not what you're used to.'

Serena thought of the Spartan conditions of the rehab facility she'd been in in England for a year, and then of her tiny studio apartment in a very insalubrious part of Athens. She smiled sweetly. 'How would you know?'

Luca scowled then. 'You're determined to stay in Rio?'

Never more so than right now. Even if just to annoy this man. 'Yes.'

Luca looked as though he would cheerfully throttle her. 'The last thing I need right now is some eagle-eyed reporter spotting you out and about, clubbing or shopping.'

Serena bit back a sharp retort. He had no idea what her life was like now. Clubbing? Shopping? She couldn't imagine anything worse.

Her smile got even sweeter. 'I'll wear a Louis Vuitton bag over my head while I go shopping for the latest Chanel suit. Will that help?'

That didn't go down well. Blood throbbed visibly in Luca's temple. 'You leaving Rio would be an even bigger help.'

Serena unconsciously mimicked his wide-legged stance. 'Well, unless you're planning on forcibly re-moving me, that's not going to happen. And if you even try such a thing I'll call the police and tell them you're harassing me.'

Luca didn't bother to tell her that with far greater problems in the city the police would no doubt just ogle her pale golden beauty before sending her on her way. And that such a stunt would only draw the interest of the paparazzi, who followed him most days.

The very thought of her being spotted, identified and linked to him was enough to make him go cold inside. He'd had enough bad press and innuendo after what had happened in Italy to last him a lifetime.

An audacious idea was being formulated in his head. It wasn't one he particularly relished, but it seemed like the only choice he had right now. It would get Ser-ena DePiero out of Rio more or less immediately, and hopefully out of Brazil entirely within a couple of days.

'You said earlier that you were looking for another chance? That you'd do anything?'

Serena went very still, those huge blue eyes narrow-ing on him. Irritation made Luca's skin feel tight. The room was too small. All he could see was her. When she'd dropped her arms his eyes had tracked hungrily to her breasts, and he could still recall the jut of those hard nipples against her T-shirt. She was naked underneath.

Blood pooled at his groin, making him hard. *Damn.*

'Do you want a chance or not?' he growled, angry at his unwarranted response. Angry that she was still here.

Serena blinked. 'Yes, of course I do.'

Her voice had become husky and it had a direct effect on Luca's arousal. This was a mistake—he knew it. But he had no choice. Damage limitation.

Tersely, he said, 'I run an ethical mining company. I'm due to visit the Iruwaya mines, and the tribe that lives near there, to check on progress. You can prove your commitment by coming with me, instead of the assistant I'd lined up, to take notes. The village is part of the global communities network, so it's not entirely unrelated.'

'Where is the village?'

'Near Manaus.'

Serena's eyes widened. 'The city in the middle of the Amazon?'

Luca nodded. Perhaps this would be all it would take? Just the thought of doing something vaguely like hard work would have her scrambling back. Giving in. Leaving.

As if to mock his line of thought, Serena looked at him with those huge blue eyes and said determinedly, 'Fine. When do we go?'

Her response surprised Luca—much as the fact that she'd chosen this rundown flea-pit of a hotel had surprised him. He'd expected her to check into one of Rio's five-star resorts. But then he'd figured that perhaps her family had her on a tight leash where funds were concerned.

Whatever. He cursed himself again for wondering about her and said abruptly, 'Tomorrow. My driver will pick you up at five a.m.'

Once again he expected her to balk, but she didn't. He swept his gaze over the minor explosion of clothes from her suitcase and the toiletries spread across the narrow bed. The fact that her scent was clean and sweet, at odds with the sultry, sexy perfume he remembered from before, was not a welcome observation.

He looked back to her. 'I'll have an assistant stop by with supplies for the trip within the hour. You won't be able to bring your case.'

That gaze narrowed again. Suspicious. 'Supplies?'

Luca faced her squarely and said, with only the slightest twinge to his conscience, 'Oh, didn't I mention that we would be trekking through the jungle to get to the village? It takes two days from the farthest outskirts of Manaus.'

Those blue eyes flashed. 'No,' she responded. 'You didn't mention that we would be trekking through the jungle. Is it even safe?'

Luca smiled, enjoying the thought of Serena bailing after half an hour of walking through the earth's largest insect and wildlife-infested hothouse. He figured that after her first brush with one of the Amazon's countless insect or animal species she'd give up the act. But for now he'd go along with it. Because if he didn't she'd be a loose cannon in Rio de Janeiro. A ticking publicity time bomb. At least this way she'd have to admit defeat and go of her own free will.

He made a mental note to have a helicopter standing by to extract her and take her to the airport.

'It's eminently safe, once you have a guide who knows what they're doing and where they're going.'

'And that's you?' she said flatly.

'Yes. I've been visiting this tribe for many years, and

exploring the Amazon for a lot longer than that. You couldn't be in safer hands.'

The look Serena shot him told him that she doubted that. His smile grew wider and he arched a brow. 'By all means you can say no, Serena, it's entirely up to you.'

She made a derisive sound. 'And if I say no you'll personally escort me to the airport, no doubt.'

She stopped and bit her lip for a moment, making Luca's awareness of her spike.

'But if I do this, and prove my commitment, will you let me take up the job I came for?'

Luca's smile faded and he regarded her. Once again that tiny grudging admiration reared its head. He ruthlessly crushed it.

'Well, as I'm almost certain you won't last two hours in the jungle it's a moot point. All this is doing is delaying your inevitable return home.'

Her chin lifted and her arms tightened over her chest. 'It'll take more than a trek and some dense vegetation to put me off, Fonseca.'

The early-morning air was sultry, and the dawn hadn't yet broken, so it was dark when Serena got out of the back of the chauffeur-driven car at the private airfield almost twelve hours later. The first person she saw was the tall figure of Luca, carrying bags into a small plane. Instantly her nerves intensified.

He barely glanced at her as she walked over behind the driver, who carried the new backpack she'd been furnished with. And then his dark gaze fell on her and her heart sped up.

'You checked out of the hotel?'

Good morning to you too, Serena said silently, and

cursed her helpless physical reaction. 'Yes. And my suitcase is in the car.'

Luca took her small backpack from the driver and exchanged a few words with him in rapid Portuguese. Then, as the driver walked away, Luca said, 'Your things will be left at my headquarters until you get back.'

The obvious implication of *you*—not *we*—was not lost on Serena, and she said coolly, 'I won't be bailing early.'

Luca looked at her assessingly and Serena was conscious of the new clothes and shoes she'd been given. Lightweight trousers and a sleeveless vest under a khaki shirt. Sturdy trekking boots. Much like what Luca was wearing, except his looked well worn, faded with time. Doing little to hide his impressive muscles and physique.

She cursed. Why did he have to be the one man who seemed to connect with her in a way she'd never felt before?

Luca, who had turned back to the plane, said over his shoulder, 'Come on, we have a flight slot to make.'

'Aye-aye, sir,' Serena muttered under her breath as she hurried after him and up the steps into the small plane. She was glad that she'd pulled her hair up into a knot on top of her head as she could already feel a light sweat breaking out on the back of her neck.

Luca told her to take a seat. He shut the heavy door and secured it.

As Serena was closing her seatbelt she saw him take his seat in the cockpit and gasped out loud, *'You're* the pilot?'

'Evidently,' he said drily.

Serena's throat dried. 'Are you even qualified?'

He was busy flicking switches and turning knobs. He threw back over his shoulder, 'Since I was eighteen. Relax, Serena.'

He put on a headset then, presumably to communicate with the control tower, and then they were taxiing down the runway. Serena wasn't normally a nervous flyer, but her hands gripped the armrests as the full enormity of what was happening hit her. She was on a plane, headed into the world's densest and most potentially dangerous ecosystem, with a man who hated her guts.

She had a vision of a snake, dropping out of a tree in front of her face, and shivered in the dry cabin air just as the small plane left the ground and soared into the dawn-filled sky. Unfortunately her spirits didn't soar with it, but she comforted herself that at least she wasn't arriving back in Athens with her tail between her legs…just yet.

Serena was very aware of Luca's broad-shouldered physique at the front of the plane, but as much as she wanted to couldn't quite drum up the antipathy she wanted to feel for him. After all, he had good reason to believe what he did about her—that she'd framed him.

Anyone else would have believed the same…except for her sister, who had just looked at her with that sad expression that had reminded Serena of how trapped they both were by their circumstances—and by Serena's helpless descent into addiction to block out the pain.

Their father had simply been too powerful. And Siena had been too young for Serena to try anything drastic like running away. By the time Siena had come of age Serena had been in no shape to do anything drastic. Their father had seen to that effectively. And they'd been too well known. Any attempt to run would have been ended within hours, because their father would have sent his goons after them. They'd been bound as effectively as if their father had locked them in a tower.

'*Serena.*'

Serena's attention came back to the small plane and she looked forward, to see Luca staring back to her impatiently. He must have called her a couple of times. She felt raw from her memories.

'What?'

'I was letting you know that the flight will take four hours.' He pointed to a bag on the floor near her and said, 'You'll find some information in there about the tribe and the mines. You should read up on them.'

He turned back to the front and Serena restrained herself from sticking her tongue out at him. She'd been bullied and controlled by one man for most of her life and she chafed at the thought of giving herself over to that treatment again.

As she dug for the documents she reiterated to herself that this was a means to an end. She'd chosen to come here with Luca, and she was going to get through it in one piece and prove herself to him if it was the last thing she did. She'd become adept in the past few years in focusing on the present, not looking back. And she'd need that skill now more than ever.

Just over four hours later Serena was feeling a little more in control of herself, and her head was bursting with information about where they were going. She was already fascinated and more excited about the trip, which felt like a minor victory in itself.

They'd landed in a private part of the airport and after a light breakfast, which had been laid out for them in a private VIP room, Luca was now loading bags and supplies into the back of a Jeep.

His backpack was about three times the size of hers. And there were walking poles. Nerves fluttered in Serena's belly. Maybe she was being really stupid. How on earth was she going to last in the jungle? She was a city girl... That was the jungle she understood and knew how to navigate.

Luca must have caught her expression and he arched a questioning brow. Instantly fresh resolve filled Serena and she marched forward. 'Is there anything I can do?'

He shut the Jeep's boot door. 'No, we're good. Let's go—we don't have all day.'

A short time later, as Luca navigated the Manaus traffic, which eventually got less crazy as they hit the suburbs, he delivered a veritable lecture to Serena on safety in the jungle.

'And whatever you do obey my commands. The jungle is perceived to be a very hostile environment, but it doesn't have to be—as long as you use your head and you're constantly on guard and aware of what's around you.'

A devil inside Serena prompted her to say, 'Are you always this bossy or is it just with me?'

To her surprise Luca's mouth lifted ever so slightly on one side, causing a reaction of seismic proportions in Serena's belly.

That dark navy glance slid to her for a second and he drawled, 'I instruct and people obey.'

Serena let out a small sound of disdain. That had

been her father's philosophy too. 'That must make life very boring.'

The glimmer of a smile vanished. 'I find that people are generally compliant when it's in their interests to gain something...as you yourself are demonstrating right now.'

There was an unmistakably cynical edge to his voice that had Serena's gaze fixed on his face. Not liking the fact that she'd noticed it, and wondering about where such cynicism stemmed from, she said, 'You offered me a chance to prove my commitment. That's what I'm doing.'

He shrugged one wide shoulder. 'Exactly my point. You have something to gain.'

'Do I, though?' Serena asked quietly, but Luca either didn't hear or didn't think it worth answering. Clearly the answer was *no*.

They were silent for the rest of the journey. Soon they'd left the city behind, and civilisation was slowly swallowed by greenery until they were surrounded by it. It gave Serena a very real sense of how ready the forest seemed to be to encroach upon its concrete rival given half a chance.

Her curiosity overcame her desire to limit her interaction with Luca. 'How did you become interested in these particular mines?'

One of his hands was resting carelessly on the wheel, the other on his thigh. He was a good driver—unhurried, but fast. In control. He looked at her and she felt very conscious of being in a cocoon-like atmosphere with nothing but green around them.

He returned his attention to the road. 'My grandfather opened them up when prospectors found bauxite.

The area was plundered, forest cleared, and the native Indians moved on to allow for a camp to be set up. It was the first of my family's mines…and so the first one that I wanted to focus on to try and undo the damage.'

Serena recalled what she'd read. 'But you're still mining?'

He frowned at her and put both hands on the wheel, as if that reminder had angered him. 'Yes, but on a much smaller scale. The main camp has already been torn down. Miners commute in and out from a nearby town. If I was to shut down the mine completely it would affect the livelihoods of hundreds of people. I'd also be doing the workers out of government grants for miners, education for their children, and so on. As it is, we're using this mine as a pilot project to develop ethical mining so that it becomes the standard.'

He continued. 'The proceeds are all being funnelled into restoring huge swathes of the forest that were cleared—they'll never be restored completely, but they can be used for other ends, and the native Indians who were taken off the land have moved back to farm that land and make a new living from it.'

'It sounds like an ambitious project.' Serena tried not to feel impressed. Her experience with her father had taught her that men could be masters in the art of altruism while hiding a soul so corrupt and black it would make the devil look like Mickey Mouse.

Luca glanced at her and she could see the fire of intent in his eyes—something she'd never seen in her father's eyes unless it was for his own ends. Greedy for more power. Control. Causing pain.

'It is an ambitious project. But it's my responsibility. My grandfather did untold damage to this country's natural habitat and my father continued his reckless destruction. I refuse to keep perpetuating the same mistake. Apart from anything else, to do so is to completely ignore the fact that the planet is intensely vulnerable.'

Serena was taken aback at the passion in his voice. Maybe he *was* genuine.

'Why do you care so much?'

He tensed, and she thought he wouldn't answer, but then he said, 'Because I saw the disgust the native Indians and even the miners had for my father and men like him whenever I went with him to visit his empire. I started to do my own research at a young age. I was horrified to find out the extent of the damage we were doing—not only to our country but on a worldwide scale—and I was determined to put an end to it.'

Serena looked at his stern profile, unable to stem her growing respect. Luca was turning the Jeep into an opening that was almost entirely hidden from view. The track was bumpy and rough, the huge majestic trees of the rainforest within touching distance now.

After about ten minutes of solid driving, deeper and deeper into the undergrowth, they emerged into a large clearing where a two-storey state-of-the-art facility was revealed, almost completely camouflaged to blend with the surroundings.

Luca brought the Jeep to a halt alongside a few other vehicles. 'This is our main Amazon operational research base. We have other smaller ones in different locations.' He looked at her before he got out of the Jeep. 'You should take this opportunity to use the facilities while we still have them.'

Serena wanted to scowl at the very definite glint of mockery in his eyes but she refused to let him see the flicker of trepidation she felt once again, when confronted with the reality of their awe-inspiring surroundings.

She was mesmerised by the dense foliage around them. She had that impression again that the forest was being held back by sheer will alone, as if given the slightest chance it would extend its roots and vines and overtake this place.

'Serena?'

Frowning impatiently, Luca was holding open the main door.

She walked in and he pointed down a corridor.

'The bathroom is down there. I'll meet you back here.'

When Serena found the bathroom and saw her own reflection in dozens of mirrors, she grimaced. She looked flushed and sweaty, and was willing to bet that if she made it to the end of the day she'd look a lot worse.

After throwing some water on her face and tying her hair back into a more practical plait she headed back, nerves jumping around in her belly at the prospect of the battle of wills ahead and her determination not to falter at the first hurdle.

When Serena joined Luca back outside he handed her the backpack. There was a long rubber hose coming from the inside of it to sit over one shoulder. He saw her look at it.

'That's your water supply. Sip little and often; we'll replenish it later.'

She put the pack on and secured it around her waist and over her chest. She was relieved to find that it didn't feel too heavy at all. And then she saw the size of

Luca's pack, which obviously held all their main supplies and had a tent rolled up at the bottom.

Her eyes widened when she saw what looked suspiciously like a gun in a holster on his waist. He saw her
expression and commented drily, 'It's a tranquilliser
gun.' He sent a thorough glance up and down her body
and remarked, 'Tuck your trousers into your socks and
make sure your shirtsleeves are down and the cuffs
closed.'

Feeling more and more nervous, Serena did as he
said. When she looked at him again, feeling like a child
about to be inspected in her school uniform, he was
cocking a dark brow over those stunning eyes.

'Are you sure about this? Now would be a really good
time to say no, if that's your intention.'

Serena put her hands on her hips and hid every one
of her nerves behind bravado. 'I thought you said we
don't have all day?'

CHAPTER THREE

A COUPLE OF hours later Serena was blindingly aware only of stepping where Luca stepped—which was a challenge, when his legs were so much longer. Her breath was wheezing in and out of her straining lungs. Rivers of sweat ran from every pore in her body.

She was soaked through. And it was no consolation to see sweat patches showing on Luca's body too, because they only seemed to enhance his impressive physicality.

She hadn't known what to expect, what the rainforest would be like, but it was more humid than she'd ever imagined it could be. And it was *loud*. Screamingly loud. With about a dozen different animal and bird calls at any time. She'd looked up numerous times to see a glorious flash of colour as some bird she couldn't name flew past, and had once caught sight of monkeys high in the canopy, loping lazily from branch to branch.

It was an onslaught on her senses, and Serena longed to stop for a minute to try and assimilate it all, but she didn't dare say a word to Luca, who hadn't stopped since he strode into the jungle, expecting her to follow him. He'd sent only the most cursory of glances back—presumably to make sure she hadn't been dragged into the dense greenery by one of mythical beasts that were running rampant in her imagination.

Every time the undergrowth rustled near her she sped up a little. Consequently, when Luca stopped suddenly and turned, Serena almost ran into him and skidded to a halt only just in time.

She noticed belatedly that they were on the edge of a clearing. It was almost a relief to get out of the oppressive atmosphere of the forest and suck in some breaths. She put her hands on her hips and hoped she didn't look as if she was about to burst a blood vessel.

Luca extracted something from a pocket in his trousers. It looked like a slightly old-fashioned mobile phone, a little larger than the current models.

'This is a satellite phone. I can call the chopper and it'll be here in fifteen minutes. This is your last chance to walk away.'

On the one hand Serena longed for nothing more than to see the horizon fill up with a cityscape again. And to feel the blast of clean, cool water on her skin. She was boiling. Sweating. And her muscles were burning. But, perversely, she'd never felt more energised, in spite of the debilitating heat. And, apart from anything else, she had a fierce desire to show no weakness to this man. He was the only thing that stood between her and independence.

'I'm not going anywhere, Luca.'

A glimpse of something distinctly like surprise crossed his face, and a dart of pleasure made Serena stand tall. Even that small indication that she was proving to be not as easy a pushover as he'd clearly expected was enough to keep her rooted to the spot.

He looked down then, his attention taken by something, and then back up at her. A very wicked hint of a smile was playing about his mouth as he said, with a pointed look towards her feet, 'Are you absolutely sure?'

Serena looked down and her whole body froze with fear and terror when she saw a small black scorpion crawling over the toe of her boot with its tail curled high over its arachnid body.

Without any previous experience of anything so potentially dangerous, Serena fought down the fear and took her walking pole and gently nudged the scorpion off her shoe. It scuttled off into the undergrowth. Feeling slightly light-headed at what she'd just done, she looked back at Luca.

'Like I said, I'm not going anywhere.'

Luca couldn't stem a flash of respect. Not many others would have reacted to seeing a scorpion like that with such equanimity. Men included. And any woman he knew would have used it as an excuse to hurl herself into his arms, squeaking with terror.

But Serena was staring him down. Blue eyes massive. Something in his chest clenched for a moment, making him short of breath. In spite of being sweaty and dishevelled, she was still stunningly beautiful. Helen of Troy beautiful. He could appreciate in that moment how men could be driven to war or driven mad because of the beauty of one woman.

But not him.

Not when he knew first-hand just how strong her sense of self-preservation was. Strong enough to let another take the fall for her own misdeeds.

'Fine,' he declared reluctantly. 'Then let's keep going.'

He turned his back on the provocative view of a flushed-faced Serena and strode back into the jungle.

Serena sucked in a few last deep breaths, relishing the cleared space for the last time, and then followed Luca, unable to stem the surge of triumph that he was letting her stay. And as she followed him she tried not to wince at the way her boots were pinching at her ankles and toes, pushing all thoughts of pain out of her head. Here, she couldn't afford to be weak. Luca would seize on it like a predator wearing its quarry down to exhaustion.

Serena felt as if she was floating above her body slightly. Pain was affecting so many parts of her that it had all coalesced into one throbbing beat of agony. Her backpack, which had been light that morning, now felt as if someone had been adding wet sand to it while she walked.

They'd stopped only briefly and silently for a few minutes while Luca had doled out a protein bar and some figs he'd pulled from a nearby tree—which had incidentally tasted delicious. And then they'd kept going.

Her feet were mercifully numb after going through the pain barrier some time ago. Her throat was parched, no matter how much water she sipped, and her legs were like jelly. But Luca's pace was remorseless. And Serena was loath to call out with so much as a whisper.

And then he stopped, suddenly, and looked around him, holding up a compass. He glanced back at her and said, 'Through here—stick close to me.'

She followed where he led for a couple of minutes, and then cannoned into his backpack and gave a little yelp of surprise when he stopped again abruptly. He turned and steadied her with his big hands. Serena hadn't even realised she was swaying until he did that.

'This is the camp.'

Serena blinked. Luca took his hands away and she didn't like how aware she was of that lack of touch.

Afraid he might see something she didn't want him to, she stepped back.

'Camp?'

She looked around and saw a small but obviously well-used clearing. She also noticed belatedly that the cacophony that had accompanied them all day had silenced now, and it was as if an expectant hush lay over the whole forest. The intense heat was lessening slightly.

'It's so quiet.'

'You won't be saying that in about half an hour, when the night chorus starts up.' He was unloading his backpack and said over his shoulder, 'Take yours off too.'

Serena let it drop from her aching body and almost cried out with the relief. She felt as though she might lift right out of the forest now that the heavy weight was gone.

Luca was down on his haunches, extracting things from his bag, and the material of his trousers was drawn taut over his powerful thighs. Serena found it hard to drag her gaze away, not liking the spasm of awareness in her lower belly.

He was unrolling the tent, which looked from where Serena was standing alarmingly *small*. Oblivious to her growing horror, Luca efficiently erected the lightweight structure with dextrous speed.

When the full enormity of its intimate size sank in, Serena said in a hoarse voice, 'We're not sleeping in that.'

Luca looked up from where he was driving a stake into the ground with unnecessary force. 'Oh, yes, *we* are, *minha beleza*—that is unless you'd prefer to take your chances sleeping al fresco? Jaguars are prevalent in this area. I'm sure they'd enjoy feasting on your fragrant flesh.'

Tension, fear and panic at the thought of sharing such a confined space with him spiked in Serena as Luca straightened up. She put her hands on her hips. 'You're lying.'

Luca looked at her, impossibly dark and dangerous. 'Do you really want to take that chance?' He swept an arm out. 'By all means be my guest. But if the jaguars don't get you any number of thousands of insects will do the job—not to mention bats. While you're thinking about that I'm going to replenish our water supplies.'

He started to leave and then stopped.

'While I'm gone you could take out some tinned food and set up the camping stove.'

When he walked away Serena had to resist the cowardly urge to call out that she'd go with him. She was sure he was just scaring her. Even so, she looked around nervously and stuck close to the tent as she did as he'd instructed, muttering to herself under her breath about how arrogant he was.

When Luca returned, a short while later, Serena was standing by the tent, clearly waiting for his return with more than a hint of nervousness. He stopped in his tracks, hidden behind a tree. His conscience pricked him for having scared her before. And something else inside him sizzled. *Desire*.

His gaze wandered down and took in the clothes that were all but plastered to her body after a day of trekking through the most humid ecosystem on earth. Her body was clearly defined and she was all woman, with firm, generous breasts, a small waist and curvaceous hips.

The whole aim of bringing her here had been to make her run screaming in the opposite direction, as far away as possible from him, but she'd been with him all the way.

He could still recall the terror tightening her face when she'd seen the scorpion and yet she hadn't allowed it to rise. He'd pursued a punishing pace today, even for him, and yet every time he'd cast a glance back she'd been right there, on his heels, dogged, eyes down, assiduously watching where she stepped as he'd instructed. Sweat had dripped down over her jaw and neck, making him think of it trickling into the lush valley of her breasts, dewing her golden skin with moisture.

Damn her. He hated to admit that up to now he'd been viewing her almost as a temporary irritation—like a tick that would eventually fall off his skin and leave him alone—but she was proving to be annoyingly resilient. He certainly hadn't expected to be sharing his tent with her.

The Serena DePiero he'd pegged as a reckless and wild party girl out only for herself was the woman he'd expected. The one he'd expected to leave Rio de Janeiro as soon as she'd figured she was on a hiding to nothing.

But she hadn't left.

So who the hell was the woman waiting for him now, if she wasn't the spoiled heiress? And why did he even care?

Serena bit her lip. The light was fading fast and there was no sign of Luca returning. She felt intensely vulnerable right then, and never more aware of her puny insignificance in the face of nature's awesome grandeur and power. A grandeur that would sweep her aside in a second if it had half a chance.

And then the snap of a twig alerted her to his presence. He loomed out of the gloom, dark and powerful. Sheer, abject relief that she wasn't alone made her feel momentarily dizzy, before she reminded herself that she really hated him for scaring her earlier.

Luca must have caught something of her relief. 'Worried that I'd got eaten by a jaguar, princess?'

'One can but hope,' Serena said sweetly, and then scowled. 'And don't call me princess.'

Luca brushed past her and took in the camping stove, commenting, 'I see you can follow instructions, at least.'

Serena scowled even more, irritated that she'd done his bidding. Luca was now gathering up wood and placing it in a small clearing not far from the tent. Determined not to let him see how much he rattled her, she said perkily, 'Can I help?'

Luca straightened from dumping some wood. 'You could collect some wood—just make sure it's not alive before you pick it up.'

Serena moved around, carefully kicking pieces of twigs and wood before she picked anything up. One twig turned out to be a camouflaged beetle of some sort that scuttled off and almost made her yelp out loud.

When she looked to see if Luca had noticed, though, he was engrossed in building up an impressive base of large logs for the fire. It was dusk now, and the massive trees loomed like gigantic shadows all around them.

Serena became aware of the rising sound of the forest around them as the night shift of wildlife took over from the day shift. It grew and grew to almost deafening proportions—like a million crickets going off at once right beside her head before settling to a more harmonious hum.

She brought the last of the wood she'd collected over to the pile just as Luca bent down to set light to the fire, which quickly blazed high. Feeling was returning to her feet and they had started to throb painfully.

Luca must have seen something cross her face, because he asked curtly, 'What is it?'

With the utmost reluctance Serena said, 'It's just some blisters.'

Luca stood up. 'Come here—let me see them.'

The flickering flames made golden light dance over his shadowed face. For a second Serena was too transfixed to move. He was the most beautiful man she'd ever seen. With an effort she looked away. 'I'm sure it's nothing. Really.'

'Believe me, I'm not offering because I genuinely care what happens to you. If you have blisters and they burst then they could get infected in this humidity. And then you won't be able to walk, and I really don't plan on carrying you anywhere.'

Fire raced up Serena's spine. 'Well, when you put it so eloquently, I'd hate to become more of a burden than I already am.'

Luca guided her towards a large log near the fire. Sitting her down, he went down on his knees and pulled his bag towards him.

'Take off your boots.' His voice was gruff.

Serena undid her laces and grimaced as she pulled off the boots. Luca pulled her feet towards him, resting them on his thighs. The feel of rock-hard muscles under her feet made scarlet heat rush up through her body and bloom on her face.

She got out a strangled, 'What are you doing?'

Luca was curt. 'I'm trained as a medic—relax.'

Serena shut her mouth. She felt churlish; was there no end to his talents? She watched as he opened up a complicated-looking medical kit and couldn't help asking, 'Why did you train as a medic?'

He glanced at her swiftly before looking down again. 'I was on a visit to a village near a mine with my father when I was younger and a small boy started choking. No one knew what to do. He died right in front of us.'

Serena let out a breath. 'That's awful.'

A familiar but painful memory intruded before she could block it out. She'd seen someone die right in front of her too—it was seared onto her brain like a tattoo. Her defences didn't seem to be so robust here, in such close proximity to this man. She could empathise with Luca's helplessness and that shocked her…to feel an affinity.

Luca was oblivious to the turmoil being stirred up inside Serena with that horrific memory of her own. He continued. 'Not as awful as the fact that my father didn't let it stop him from moving the tribe on to another location, barely allowing the parents time to gather up their son's body. They were nothing to him—a problem to be got rid of.'

He was pulling down Serena's socks now, distracting her from his words and the bitterness she could hear in his voice. He sucked in a breath when he saw the angry raw blisters.

'That's my fault.'

Serena blinked. Had Luca just said that? And had he

sounded ever so slightly apologetic? Together with his obvious concern for others, it made her uncomfortable.

He looked at her, face unreadable. 'New boots. They weren't broken in. It's no wonder you've got blisters. You must have been in agony for hours.'

Serena shrugged minutely and looked away, self-conscious under his searing gaze. 'I'm no martyr, Luca. I just didn't want to delay you.'

'The truth is,' he offered somewhat sheepishly, 'I hadn't expected you to last this far. I would have put money on you opting out well before we'd even left Rio.'

Something light erupted inside Serena and for a moment their eyes met and locked. Her insides clenched hard and all she was aware of was how powerful Luca's muscles felt under her feet. He looked away then, to get something from the medical box, and the moment was broken. But it left Serena shaky.

His hands were big and capable. Masculine. But they were surprisingly gentle as he made sure the blisters were clean and then covered them with thick plasters.

He was pulling her socks back up over the dressings when he said, with an edge to his voice, 'You've said a couple of times that you didn't do drugs... You forget that I was there. I saw you.'

His blue gaze seemed to sear right through her and his question caught Serena somewhere very raw. For a moment she'd almost been feeling *soft* towards him, when he was the one who had marched her into the jungle like some kind of recalcitrant prisoner.

Anger and a sense of claustrophobia made her tense. He'd seen only the veneer of a car crash lifestyle which had hidden so much more.

She was bitter. 'You saw what you wanted to see.'

Serena avoided his eyes and reached for her boots, but Luca got there first. He shook them out and said tersely, 'You should always check to make sure nothing has crawled inside.'

Serena repressed a shudder at the thought of what that might be and stuck her feet back into the boots, but Luca didn't move away.

'What's that supposed to mean? *I saw what I wanted to see.*'

Getting angry at his insistence, she glared at him. The firelight cast his face into shadow, making him seem even more dark and brooding.

He arched a brow. 'I think I have a right to know—you owe me an explanation.'

Serena's chest was tight with some unnamed emotion. The dark forest around them made her feel as if nothing existed outside of this place.

Hesitantly, she finally said, 'I wasn't addicted to Class A drugs...I've never taken a recreational drug in my life.' She tried to block out the doubtful gleam in Luca's eyes. 'But I *was* addicted to prescription medication. And to alcohol. And I'll never touch either again.'

Luca finally moved back and frowned. Serena felt as if she could breathe again. Until he asked, 'How did you get addicted to medication?'

Serena's insides curdled. This came far too close to that dark memory and all the residual guilt and fear that had been a part of her for so long. At best Luca was mildly curious; at worst he hated her. She had no desire to seek his sympathy, but a rogue part of her wanted to knock his assumptions about her a little.

'I started taking prescribed medication when I was five.'

Luca's frown deepened. 'Why? You were a child.'

His clear scepticism made Serena curse herself for being so honest. This man would never understand if she was to tell him the worst of it all. So she feigned a lightness she didn't feel and fell back on the script that her father had written for her so long ago that she couldn't remember *normal*.

She gave a small shrug and avoided that laser-like gaze. 'I was difficult. After my mother died I became hard to control. By the time I was twelve I had been diagnosed with ADHD and had been on medication for years. I became dependent on it—I liked how it made me feel.'

Luca sounded faintly disgusted. 'And your father... he sanctioned this?'

Pain gripped Serena. He'd not only sanctioned it, he'd made sure of it. She shrugged again, feeling as brittle as glass, and smiled. But it was hard. She forced herself to look at Luca. 'Like I said, I was hard to control. Wilful.'

Disdain oozed from Luca. 'Why are you so certain you're free of the addiction now?'

She tipped her chin up unconsciously. 'When my sister and I left Italy, after my father...' She stalled, familiar shame coursing through her blood along with anger. 'When it all fell apart we went to England. I checked into a rehab facility just outside London. I was there for a year. Not that it's any business of yours,' she added, immediately regretting her impulse to divulge so much.

Luca's expression was indecipherable as he stood up, and he pointed out grimly, 'I think our personal history makes it my business. You need to prove to me you can be trusted—that you will not be a drain on resources and the energy of everyone around you.'

Boots on, Serena stood up in agitation, her jaw tight with hurt and anger. She held up a hand. 'Whoa—judgemental, much? And you base this on your vast knowledge of ex-addicts?'

His narrow-minded view made Serena see red. She put her hands on her hips.

'Well?'

Tension throbbed between them as they glared at each other for long seconds. And then Luca bit out, 'I base it on an alcoholic mother who makes checking in and out of rehab facilities a recreational pastime. That's how I have a unique insight into the addict's mind. And when she's not battling the booze or the pills she's chasing her next rich conquest to fund her lifestyle.'

Serena felt sick for a moment at the derision in his voice. The evidence of just how personal his judgement was appeared entrenched in bitter experience.

Luca stepped back. 'We should eat.'

Serena's anger dissipated as she watched Luca turn away abruptly to light the camping stove near the fire. She reeled with this new knowledge of his own experience. And reeled at how much she'd told him of herself with such little prompting. She felt relieved now that she hadn't spilled her guts entirely.

No wonder he'd come down on her like a ton of bricks and believed the worst. Still…it didn't excuse him. And she told herself fiercely that she *didn't* feel a tug of something treacherous at the thought of him coping with an alcoholic parent. After all, she still bore the guilt of her sister having to deal with *her*.

Suddenly, in light of that conversation, she felt too raw to sit in Luca's company and risk that insightful mind being turned on her again. And fatigue was creeping over her like a relentless wave.

'Don't prepare anything for me. I'm not feeling hungry. I think I'll turn in now.'

Luca looked up at her from over his shoulder. He seemed to bite back whatever he was going to say and shrugged. 'Suit yourself.'

Serena grabbed her backpack and went into the tent, relieved to see that it was more spacious inside than she might have imagined. She could only do a basic toilette, and after taking off her boots and rolling out her sleeping bag carefully on one side of the tent she curled up and dived into the exhausted sleep of oblivion.

Anything to avoid thinking about the man who had comprehensively turned her world upside down in the last thirty-six hours and come far too close to where she still had so much locked away.

CHAPTER FOUR

THE FOLLOWING MORNING Luca heard movement from the tent and his whole body tensed. When he'd turned in last night Serena had been curled up in a ball inside her sleeping bag, some long hair trailing in tantalising golden strands around her head, her breathing deep and even. And once again he'd felt the sting of his conscience at knowing she'd gone to bed with no food, and her feet rubbed raw from new boots.

What she'd told him the previous evening had shocked him. She'd been taking medication since she was a child. Out of control even then. It was so at odds with the woman she seemed to be now that he almost couldn't believe it.

She'd sounded defiant when she'd told him that she'd been addicted by the age of twelve. Something inside him had recoiled with disgust at the thought. It was one thing to have a mother who was an addict as an adult. But a *child*?

Serena had given him the distinct impression that even then she'd known what she was doing and had revelled in it. But even as he thought that, something about the way she'd said it niggled at him. It didn't sit right.

Was she telling the truth?

Why would she lie after all this time? an inner voice pointed out. And if she hadn't ever done recreational drugs then maybe she really hadn't planted them on him that night... He didn't like the way the knowledge sank like a stone in his belly.

The crush and chaos of the club that night came back to him and a flash of a memory caught him unawares: Serena's hand slipping into his. He'd looked down at her and she'd been wide-eyed, her face pale. That had been just before the Italian police had separated them roughly and searched them.

The memory mocked him now. He'd always believed that look to have been Serena's guilt and pseudo-vulnerability, knowing what she'd just done. But if it hadn't been guilt it had been something far more ambiguous. It made him think of her passionate defence when he'd questioned her trustworthiness. And why on earth did that gnaw at him now? Making him feel almost guilty?

The flaps of the tent moved and the object of his thoughts emerged, blinking in the dawn light. She'd pulled her hair up into a bun on top of her head, and when that blue gaze caught his, Luca's insides tightened. He cursed her silently—and himself for bringing her here and putting questions into his head.

For possibly being innocent of the charges he'd levelled against her.

She straightened up and her gaze was wary. 'Morning.'

Her voice was sleep-rough enough to tug forcibly at Luca's simmering desire. She should look creased and dishevelled and grimy, but she looked gorgeous. Her skin was as dewy and clear as if she'd just emerged from a spa, not a night spent in a rudimentary tent in the middle of the jungle.

He thrust a bowl of protein-rich tinned food towards her. 'Here—eat this.'

There was the most minute flash of something in her eyes as she acknowledged his lack of greeting, but she took the bowl and a spoon and sat down on a nearby log to eat, barely wincing at the less than appetising meal. Yet another blow to Luca's firmly entrenched antipathy.

He looked at her and forced himself to ignore that dart of guilt he'd just felt—to remember that thanks to his mother's stellar example he knew all about the mercurial nature of addicts. How as soon as you thought they truly were intent on making a change they went and did the exact opposite. From a young age Luca had witnessed first-hand just how brutal that lack of regard could be and he'd never forgotten it.

Serena looked up at him. She'd finished her meal, and Luca felt slightly winded at the intensity of her gaze. He reached down and took the bowl and handed her a protein bar. His voice gruff, which irritated him, he said, 'Eat this too.'

'But I'm full now. I—'

Luca held it out and said tersely, 'Eat it, Serena. I can't afford for you to be weak. We have a long walk today.'

Serena's eyes flashed properly at that, and she stood up with smooth grace and took the bar from his outstretched hand. Tension bristled and crackled between them.

Serena cursed herself for thinking, *hoping* that some kind of a truce might have grown between them. And she cursed herself again for revealing what she had last night.

Luca was cleaning up the camp, packing things away, getting ready to move on. When she'd woken a while ago it had taken long seconds for her to realise where she was and with whom. A sense of exultation had rushed through her at knowing they were still in the jungle and that she'd survived the first day, that she hadn't shown Luca any weakness.

Then she'd remembered the gentleness of his hands on her feet and had felt hot. And then she'd got hotter, acknowledging that only extreme exhaustion had knocked her out enough to sleep through sharing such an intimate space with him.

Before Luca might see some of that heat in her expression or in her eyes, Serena busied herself with rolling up the sleeping bags and starting to take down the tent efficiently.

'Where did you learn to do that?' came Luca's voice, its tone incredulous.

Serena barely glanced at him, prickling. 'We used to go on camping trips while we were in rehab. It was part of the programme.'

She tensed, waiting for him to be derisive or to ask her about it, but he didn't. He just went and started unpegging the other side of the tent. Serena hadn't shared her experience of rehab with anyone—not even her sister. Even though her sister had been the one who had sacrificed almost everything to ensure Serena's care, working herself to the bone and putting herself unwittingly at the mercy of a man she'd betrayed years before and who had come looking for revenge.

Against the odds, though, Siena and Andreas had fallen in love and were now blissfully happy, with a toddler and a baby. Sometimes their intense happiness made Serena feel unaccountably alienated, and she hated herself for the weakness. But it was the same with her half-brother Rocco and his wife and children. If she'd never believed in love or genuine happiness theirs mocked her for it every time she saw them.

Without even realising it was done, she saw the camp was cleared and Luca was handing Serena her backpack.

He arched a brow. 'Ready?'

Serena took the pack and nodded swiftly, not wanting Luca to guess at the sudden vulnerability she felt to be thinking of her family and their very natural self-absorption.

She put on the pack and followed Luca for a few steps until he turned abruptly. 'How are your feet?'

Serena frowned and said, with some surprise, 'They're fine, actually.'

Luca made an indeterminate sound and carried on, and Serena tried not to fool herself that he'd asked out of any genuine concern.

As they walked the heat progressed and intensified to almost suffocating proportions. When they stopped briefly by a small stream in the afternoon Serena almost wept with relief to be able to throw some cool water over her face and head. She soaked a cloth handkerchief and tied it around her neck.

It was only a short reprieve. Luca picked up the punishing pace again, not even looking to see if Serena was behind him. Irritation rose up inside her. Would he even notice if she was suddenly pulled by some animal into the undergrowth? He'd probably just shrug and carry on.

After another hour any feeling of relief from the

stream was a distant memory and sweat dripped down
her face, neck and back. Her limbs were aching, her
feet numb again. Luca strode on, though, like some
kind of robot, and suddenly Serena felt an urge to pro-
voke him, needle him. Force him to stop and face her.
Acknowledge that she had done well to last this far.
Acknowledge that she might be telling the truth about
the drugs.

She called out, 'So, are you prepared to admit that I
might be innocent after all?'

She got her wish. Luca stopped dead in his tracks
and then, after a long second, slowly turned around.
His eyes were so dark they looked black. He covered
the space between them so fast and silently that Serena
took an involuntary step backwards, hating herself for
the reflexive action.

He looked infinitely dangerous, and yet perversely
Serena didn't feel scared. She felt something far more
ambiguous and hotter, deep in her pelvis.

'To be quite frank, I don't think I even care any more
whether or not you did it. The fact is that my involve-
ment with you made things so much worse. *You* were
enough to turn the incident into front-page news and
put certainty into people's minds about my guilt—because they all believed that *you* did drugs, and that I
was either covering for you or dealing to you. So, innocent bystander or not—as you might have been—I
still got punished.'

Serena swallowed down a sudden and very unwelcome lump in her throat. She recognised uncomfortably
that the need for this man to know she was innocent
was futile or worse. 'You'll never forgive me for it,
will you?'

His jaw clenched, and just then a huge drop of water landed on her face—so large that it splashed.

Luca looked up and cursed out loud.

'What? What is it?' Serena asked, her tension dissolving to be replaced by a tendril of fear.

Luca looked around them and bit out, 'Rain. *Damn.* I'd hoped to make the village first. We'll have to shelter. Come on.'

Even before he'd begun striding away again the rain was starting in earnest, those huge drops cascading from the sky above the canopy. Serena hurried after him to try and keep up. Within seconds, though, it was almost impossible to see a few feet in front of her nose. Genuine panic spiked. She couldn't see Luca any more. And then he reappeared, taking her hand, keeping her close.

The rain was majestic, awesome. Deafening. But Serena was only aware of her hand in Luca's. He was leading them through the trees, off the path to a small clearing. The ground was slightly higher here. He let her go and she saw him unrolling a tarpaulin. Catching on quickly, she took one end and tied it off to a nearby sapling while Luca did the same on the other side, creating a shelter a few feet off the ground.

He laid out another piece of tarpaulin under the one they'd tied off and shouted over the roar of the rain, 'Get underneath!'

Serena slipped off her pack and did so. Luca joined her seconds later. They were drenched. Steam was rising off their clothes. But they were out of the worst of the downpour. Serena was still taken aback at how quickly it had come down.

They sat like that, their breaths evening out, for

long minutes. Eventually she asked, 'How long will it last?'

Luca craned his neck to look out, his arms around his knees. He shrugged one wide shoulder. 'Could be minutes—could be hours. Either way, we'll have to camp out again tonight. The village is only a couple of hours away, but it'll be getting dark soon—too risky.'

At the thought of another night in the tent with Luca, flutters gripped Serena's abdomen. He was pulling something out of a pocket and handed her another protein bar. Serena reached for it with her palm facing up, but before she could take it Luca had grabbed her wrist and was frowning.

She was distracted by his touch for a moment—all she felt was *heat*—and then he was saying, 'What are those marks? Did you get them here?'

He was inspecting her palm and pulling her other hand towards him to look at that, too. Far too belatedly Serena panicked, and tried to pull them back, but he wouldn't let her, clearly concerned that it had happened recently.

She saw what he saw: the tiny criss-cross of old, silvery scars that laced her palms.

As if coming to that realisation, he said, 'They're old.' He looked at her, stern. '*How* old?'

Serena tried to jerk her hands away but he held them fast. Her breath was choppy now, with a surge of emotion. And with anger that he was quizzing her as if she'd done something wrong.

She said reluctantly, 'They're twenty-two years old.'

Luca looked at her, turning towards her. '*Deus*, what *are* they?'

Serena was caught by his eyes. They blazed into hers,

seeking out some kind of truth and justice—which she was coming to realise was integral to this man's nature. It made him see the world in black and white, good and bad. And she was firmly in the bad category as far as he was concerned.

But just for once, Serena didn't want to be. She felt tired. Her throat ached with repressed emotions, with all the horrific images she held within her head, known only to her and her father. And he'd done his best to eradicate them.

A very weak and rogue part of her wanted to tell Luca the truth—much like last night—in some bid to make him see that perhaps things weren't so black and white. And even though an inner voice told her to protect herself from his derision, she heard the words spill out.

'They're the marks of a bamboo switch. My father favoured physical punishment.'

Luca's hands tightened around hers and she held back a wince. His voice was low. 'How old were you?'

Serena swallowed. 'Five—nearly six.'

'What the hell….?'

Luca's eyes burned so fiercely for a moment that Serena quivered inwardly. She took advantage of the moment to pull her hands back, clasping them together, hiding the permanent stain of her father's vindictiveness.

Serena could understand Luca's shock. Her therapist had been shocked when she'd told *her*.

She shrugged. 'He was a violent man. If I stepped out of line, or if Siena misbehaved, I'd be punished.'

'You were a *child*.'

Serena looked at Luca and felt acutely exposed, recalling just how her childhood had been so spectacularly snatched away from her, by far worse than a few scars on her palms.

She noticed something then, and seized on it weakly. 'The rain—it's stopped.'

Luca just looked at her for a long moment, as if he hadn't ever seen her before. It made Serena nervous and jittery.

Eventually he said, 'We'll make camp here. Let's set it up.'

Serena scrambled inelegantly out from under their makeshift shelter. The jungle around them was steaming from the onslaught of precipitation. It was unbearably humid…and uncomfortably sultry.

As she watched, Luca uncoiled himself, and for a moment Serena was mesmerised by his sheer masculine grace. He looked at her too quickly for her to look away.

He frowned. 'What is it?'

Serena swallowed as heat climbed up her chest. She blurted out the first thing she could think of. 'Thirsty—I'm just thirsty.'

Luca glanced around them and then strode to a nearby tree and tested the leaves. 'Come here.'

Not sure what to expect, Serena walked over. Luca put a hand on her arm and it seemed to burn right through the material.

He manoeuvred her under the leaf and said, 'Tip your head back—open your mouth.'

Serena looked at him and something dark lit his eyes, making her belly contract.

'Come on. It won't bite.'

So she did, and Luca tipped the leaf so that a cascade of water fell into her mouth, cold and more refreshing than anything she'd ever tasted in her life. She coughed slightly when it went down the wrong way, but couldn't stop her mouth opening for more. The water trickled over her face, cooling the heat that had nothing to do with the humid temperature.

When there were only a few drops left, she straightened up again. Luca was watching her. They were close—close enough that all Serena would have to do would be to step forward and they'd be touching.

And then, as if reading her mind and rejecting her line of thought, Luca stepped back, letting her arm go. 'We need to change into dry clothes.'

He walked away and Serena felt ridiculously exposed and shaky. What was *wrong* with her?

Luca was taking clothes out of his pack. He straightened up and his hands went to his shirt, undoing the buttons with long fingers. A sliver of dark muscled chest was revealed, the shadow of chest hair. And Serena was welded to the spot. She couldn't breathe.

Finally sense returned. Her face hot with embarrassment, she hurried to her own bag and concentrated on digging out her own change of clothes. The last thing she needed was to let Luca Fonseca into the deepest recesses of her psyche. But, much to her irritation, she couldn't forget the way he'd looked when he'd held her hands out for inspection, or the look in his eyes just now, when she fancied she'd seen something carnal in their depths, only for him to mock her for her fanciful imagination.

Luca was feeling more and more disorientated as he pulled on fresh clothes with rough hands. *Deus.* He'd almost backed Serena into the tree just now and covered her open mouth with his, jealous of the rainwater trickling between those plump lips.

And what about those scars on her hands? The silvery marks criss-crossing the delicate pale skin? He hadn't been prepared for the surge of panic when he'd seen them—afraid she'd been marked by something on the trail—or the feeling of rage when she'd told him so flatly who had done it.

He'd met her father once or twice at social events and had never liked the man. He had cold, dead dark eyes, and the superior air of someone used to having everything he wanted.

He didn't like to admit it, but the knowledge that he'd been violent didn't surprise Luca. He could picture the man being vindictive. Malevolent. But to his own daughters? The blonde, blue-eyed heiresses everyone had envied?

Luca knew Serena was changing behind him. He could hear the soft sounds of clothes being taken off and dropped. And then there was silence for a long moment. Telling himself it was concern, but knowing that it stemmed from a much deeper desire, Luca turned around.

Her back was to him and her legs were revealed in all their long shapely glory as she stripped off her trousers. High-cut pants showed off a toned length of thigh. Firm but curvy buttocks. When she stripped down to her bra he wanted to go over and undo it, slip his hands around her front to cup the generous swells and feel her arch into him.

He was rewarded with a burgeoning erection within seconds—no better than a pre-teen ogling a woman dressing in a changing room.

The snap of her belt around her hips broke Luca out of his trance and, angry with himself, he turned away and pulled on his own trousers. The light was falling rapidly now, and Luca had been so fixated on Serena that he was risking not having the camp set up in time.

But when he turned around again, about to issue a curt command, the words died on his lips. To his surprise Serena was already unrolling the tent and staking it out, her long ponytail swinging over her shoulder.

He cursed her silently, because he was losing his footing with this woman—fast.

Serena was sitting on a log on the opposite side of the fire to Luca a short time later, after they'd eaten their meagre meal. The tent stood close by, and she couldn't stop a surge of ridiculous pride that she'd put it up herself. He'd expected her to flee back to civilisation at the slightest hint of work or danger, but here she was, day two and surviving—if not thriving. The feeling was heady, and it made her relish her newfound independence even more.

However, none of that could block out the mortification when she thought of earlier and how close she'd come to betraying her desire for him...

She caught Luca's eye across the flickering light of the fire and he asked, 'What's the tattoo on your back?'

She went still. He must have seen the small tattoo that sat just above her left shoulderblade earlier, when she'd been changing. The thought of him looking at her made her feel hot.

The tattoo was so personal to her, she didn't want to tell him. Reluctantly, she finally said, 'It's a swallow. The bird.'

'Any significance?'

Serena almost laughed. As if she'd divulge *that* to him! He'd definitely fall off his log laughing.

She shrugged. 'It's my favourite bird. I got it done a few years ago.' *The day she'd walked out of the rehab clinic, to be precise.*

She avoided Luca's gaze. Swallows represented resurrection and rebirth... Luca would hardly look that deeply into its significance, but still... She had the uncanny sense that he might and she didn't like it.

She really wanted to avoid any more probing into her life or her head. She stood up abruptly, making Luca look up, his dark gaze narrowing on her. 'I'm going to turn in now.' She sounded too husky. Even now her body trembled with awareness, just from looking at his large rangy form relaxed.

Luca stirred the fire, oblivious to her heated imaginings. 'I'll let you get settled.'

Serena turned away and crawled into the tent, pulling off her boots, but leaving her clothes on. Then she felt silly. Luca hadn't given her the slightest hint that he felt any desire for her whatsoever, and she longed to feel cooler. She took off her shirt and stripped down to her panties, and pulled the sleeping bag around her.

She prayed that sleep would come as it had last night, like a dark blanket of oblivion, so she wouldn't have to hear Luca come in and deal with the reality that he slept just inches away from her and probably resented every moment.

Luca willed his body to cool down. He didn't like how off-centre Serena was pushing him. Making him desire her; wonder about her. Wanting to know more. She was surprising him.

He'd been exposed to the inherent selfishness of his mother and women in general from a very early age, so it was not a welcome sensation thinking that he might have misjudged her.

Lovers provided him with physical relief and an escort when he needed it. But his life was not about women, or settling down. He had too much to do to undo all the harm his father and grandfather had caused. He had set himself a mammoth task when his father had died ten years ago: to reverse the negative impact of the name Fonseca in Brazil, which up till then had been synonymous with corruption, greed and destruction.

The allegations of his drug-taking had come at the worst possible time for Luca—just when people had been beginning to sit up and trust that perhaps he *was* different and genuine about making a change. It was only now that he was back in that place.

And the person who could reverse all his good work was only feet away from him. He had to remember that. Remember who she was and what she had the power to do to him. Even if she *was* innocent, any association with her would incite all that speculation again.

Only when Luca felt sure that Serena must be asleep did he turn in himself, doing his best to ignore the curled-up shape inside the sleeping bag that was far too close to his for comfort. He'd really *not* expected to have to share this tent with anyone, and certainly not with Serena DePiero for a second night in a row.

But as he lay down beside her he had to acknowledge uncomfortably that there was no evidence of the spoilt ex-wild-child. There wasn't one other woman he could think of, apart from those whose life's work it was to study the Amazon, who would have fared better than her over the past couple of days. And even some of those would have run screaming long before now, back to the safety of a research lab, or similar.

He thought of her putting up the tent, her tongue caught between her teeth as she exerted herself, sweat dripping down her neck and disappearing into the tantalising vee of her shirt. Gritting his jaw tightly, Luca sighed and closed his eyes. He'd accused her of not lasting in the jungle, but it was he who craved the order of civilisation again—anything to dilute this fire in his blood and put an end to the questions Serena kept throwing up.

A couple of hours later Luca woke, instantly alert and tensed, waiting to hear a sound outside. But it came from inside the tent. *Serena*. Moaning in her sleep in Italian.

'Papa...no, per favore, non che... Siena, aiutami.'

Luca translated the last word: *help me*. There was something gutturally raw about her words, and they were full of pain and emotion. Her voice cracked then, and Luca's chest squeezed when he heard her crying.

Acting on instinct, Luca reached over and touched her shoulder.

Almost instantly she woke up and turned her head. *'Ché cosa?'*

Something about the fact that she was still speaking Italian made his chest tighten more. 'You were dreaming.' He felt as if he'd invaded her privacy.

Serena went as tense as a board. He could see the bright glitter of those blue eyes in the gloom.

'Sorry for waking you.'

Her voice was thick, her accent stronger. He felt her pull abruptly away from his hand as she curled up again. Her hair was a bright sliver of white-gold and his body grew hot as he thought of it trailing over his naked chest as she sat astride him and took him deep into her body.

Anger at the wanton direction of his thoughts, at how easily she got under his skin and how she'd pulled away just now, almost as if he'd done something wrong, made him say curtly, 'Serena?'

She said nothing, and that wound him up more. A moment ago he'd been feeling sorry for her, disturbed by the gut-wrenching sound of those sobs. But now memories of his mother and how she'd use her emotions to manipulate the people around her made Luca curse himself for being so weak.

It made his voice harsh. 'What the hell was *that* about?'

Her voice sounded muffled. 'I said I was sorry for waking you. It was nothing.'

'It didn't sound like nothing to me.'

Serena turned then, those eyes flashing, her hair bright against the dark backdrop of the tent. She said tautly, 'It was a dream, okay? Just a bad dream and I've already forgotten it. Can we go to sleep now, please?'

Luca reacted viscerally to the fact that Serena was all but spitting at him, clearly in no need of comfort whatsoever. She pressed his buttons like no one else, and all he could think about right then was how much he wanted her to submit to him—anything to drown out all the contradictions she was putting in his head.

He reached out and found her arms, pulled her into him, hearing her shocked little gasp.

'Luca, what are you doing?'

But the defensive tartness was gone out of her voice.

He pulled her in closer, the darkness wrapping around them but failing to hide that bright blue gaze or the gold of her hair. The slant of her stunning cheekbones.

She wasn't pulling away.

Luca's body was on fire. From somewhere he found his voice and it sounded coarse, rough. 'What am I doing?'

'This…'

And then he pulled her right into him and his mouth found hers with unerring precision. Her breasts swelled against his chest—in outrage? He didn't know, because he was falling over the very thin edge of his control.

When he felt her resistance give way after an infinitesimal moment, triumph surged through his body. He couldn't think any more, because he was swept up in the decadent darkness of a kiss that intoxicated him and reminded him of only one other similar moment… with her…seven years before.

CHAPTER FIVE

SERENA WAS STILL in shock at finding herself in Luca's arms with his mouth on hers. When he'd woken her at first, she'd had an almost overwhelming instinctive need to burrow close to him, the tentacles of that horrible nightmare clinging like slimy vines to her hot skin.

And then she'd realised just who she was with—just who was precipitating such weak feelings of wanting to seek strength and comfort. Luca Fonseca, of all people? And that dream... She hadn't had it for a long time—not since she'd been in rehab. And to be having it again, *here*, was galling. As if she was going backwards. Not forwards. And it was all his fault, for getting under her skin.

Fresh anger made her struggle futilely against Luca's superior strength even after she'd let the hot tide of desire take her over, revealing how much she wanted him. She pulled back, ripping her mouth from his, mortified to find herself breathing harshly, her breasts moving rapidly against the steel wall of his chest, nipples tight and stinging.

Her body and her mind seemed to be inhabiting two different people. Her body was saying *Please don't stop* and her head was screaming *Stop now!*

'What is it, *minha beleza?'*

The gravelly tone of Luca's voice rubbed along her nerve-endings, setting them alight. Traitors.

'Do you really think this is a good idea?'

Dammit. She sounded as if she wanted him to convince her that it was, her voice all breathy.

His eyes were like black pits in his face and Serena was glad she couldn't make out their expression. She half expected Luca to come to his senses and recoil, but instead he seemed to move even closer. His hands slipped down her arms and came around her back, making her feel quivery at how light his touch was—and yet it burned.

'Luca...?'

'Hmm...?'

His mouth came close again and his lips feathered a kiss to her neck. Liquid fire spread through Serena's pelvis. *Damn him.*

She swallowed, her body taking over her mind, making her move treacherously closer to that huge hard body.

'I don't think this is a good idea. We'll regret it.'

Luca pulled back for a moment and said throatily, 'You think too much.'

And then he was covering her mouth with his again, and any last sliver of defence or righteous anger at how vulnerable he made her feel drained away. She was drowning in his strength. Mouth clinging to his, skin tightening all over as he coaxed her lips apart to explore deeper with his tongue. His kiss seven years ago had seared itself onto her memory like a brand. This was like being woken from a deep sleep. She'd never really enjoyed kissing or being touched by men...until him. And now this.

Barely aware of the fact that Luca was pulling down the zips of their sleeping bags, she only knew that there was nothing between them now, and that he was pulling her on top of him so her breasts were crushed against his broad chest.

Both hands were on her head, fingers thrust deep into her hair, and Luca positioned her so that he could plunder her mouth with devastating skill. Serena could feel herself getting damp between her legs.

Luca drew back for a moment and Serena opened her eyes, breathing heavily. With a smooth move he manoeuvred them so that Serena was on her back and loomed over her. He looked wild, feral. Exactly the way she imagined the marauding Portuguese *conquistadores* must have looked when they'd first walked on this land.

He smoothed some hair behind her ear and Serena's breath grew choppier. Her fingers itched to touch him, to feel that chest, so when his head lowered to hers again her hands went to the buttons of his shirt and undid them, sliding in to feel the dense musculature of his chest.

She was unable to hold back a deep sound of satisfaction as her hands explored, revelling in his strength. She dragged her fingers over his chest, sliding over the ridges of his muscles, a nail grazing a flat hard nipple. Her mouth watered. She wanted to taste it.

His beard tickled her slightly, but that was soon forgotten as his tongue thrust deep, making her arch up against him. He was pulling down the strap of her vest, taking with it her bra strap, exposing the slope of her breast.

When Luca pulled back again she was gasping for breath. She looked up, but everything was blurry for a moment. She could feel Luca's fingers reach inside the lace cup of her bra, brushing enticingly close to where her nipple was so hard it ached. He pulled it down and Serena felt her breast pop free of the confinement. Luca's gaze was so hot she could feel it on her bare skin.

He breathed out. '*Perfeito...*'

His head came down, and with exquisite finesse he flicked his tongue against that tip, making Serena's breath catch and her hips move of their own volition. He flicked it again, and then slowly expored the hard flesh, before placing his whole mouth around it and suckling roughly.

Serena cried out. Her hands were on his head, in his hair. She'd never felt anything like this in her life. Sex had been something to block out, to endure, an ineffective form of escape...not something to revel in like this.

His hand was on her trousers now, undoing her button, lowering the zip. There was no hesitation. She wanted this with an all-consuming need she'd never experienced before. His hand delved under her panties as his mouth still tortured her breast.

When his fingers found the evidence of her desire he tore his mouth away. She could see his eyes glitter almost feverishly as he stroked her intimately, releasing her damp heat. Serena whimpered softly, almost mindless, her hips jerking with reaction.

'You want me.'

His words sliced through the fever in her brain.

Serena bit her lip. She was afraid to speak, afraid of what might spill out. Luca was a master torturer. With his hand he forced her legs apart as much as they could go, and then he thrust a finger deep inside, where she was slick and hot. She gasped.

'Say it, Serena.'

He sounded fierce now, his finger moving intimately against her. *Oh, God…* She was going to come. Like this. In a tent in the middle of nowhere. Just from this man touching her…

Feeling vulnerable far too late, Serena tried to bring her legs together—but Luca wouldn't let her. She could see the determination on his face. The lines stark with desire and hunger. One finger became two, stretching her, filling her. She gasped, her hands going to his shoulders.

The heel of his hand put exquisite pressure on her clitoris. She was unable to stop her hips from moving, rolling, seeking to assuage the incredible ache that was building. And then his fingers moved faster, deeper, making Serena's muscles tighten against him.

'Admit you want me…*dammit*. You're almost coming. *Say it*.'

Serena was wild now, hands clutching at him. He was looking down at her. She knew what was stopping the words being wrenched from her: the fact that Luca seemed so intent on pushing her over the edge when *he* appeared to be remarkably in control. The fact that she suspected he just wanted to prove his domination over her.

But she couldn't fight it. She needed it—*him*—too badly.

'I do…' she gasped out, the words torn from her as her body reached its crescendo against the relentless rhythm of Luca's wicked hand and fingers. 'I do…want you…*damn you*.'

And with those last guttural words she went as taut as a bowstring as the most indescribably pleasurable explosion racked her entire body and broke it apart into a million pieces before letting it float back together again.

Serena had orgasmed before. But never like this. With such intensity...losing herself in the process.

Luca's brain had melted into a pool of lust and heat. Serena's body was still clamping around his fingers and he ached to be embedded within her, so that the inferno in his body might be assuaged.

But something held him back—had held him back from replacing his hand with his erection. At some point he'd become aware that he needed this woman on a level that surpassed anything he'd ever known before.

And, worse, he needed to know that she felt it too. So making her admit it, making her *come*, had become some kind of battle of wills. She'd confounded him since she'd turned up in his office, just days ago, and this felt like the first time he'd been able to claw back some control. By making her lose hers.

But now, as he extricated his hand and her body jerked in reaction, it felt like an empty triumph. Luca pulled back and gritted his jaw at the way his body rejected letting Serena go. He pulled on his shirt, feeling wild. Undone.

Serena was moving, pulling her clothes together. He saw her hands shaking and wanted to snarl. Where was the insouciant, confident woman he remembered meeting that night in Florence? She bore no resemblance to this woman, who was almost *impossibly* shy.

Luca lay back, willing down the throbbing heat in his blood. Cursing the moment he'd ever laid eyes on

Serena DePiero. She went still beside him, and even that set his nerves on edge. Sizzling.

Eventually she said hesitantly, 'You didn't...'

She trailed off. But he knew what she'd meant to say, and suddenly her unbelievable hesitance pushed him over another edge. He'd cursed this woman for a long time for sending his life into turmoil, and yet again she was throwing up another facet of her suddenly chameleon-like personality. The most in control he'd felt around her since she'd come back into his life had been just now—when she'd been surrendering to him even though she'd obviously hated it.

He would have her—completely. In his bed. On his terms. Would reveal this hesitant shyness to be the sham that it was.

And then, when he'd had her, sated himself, he would be able to walk away and leave her behind for good. One thing was certain: he'd wanted her since the moment he'd laid eyes on her, and not even his antipathy for her had put a dent in that need. If he didn't have her he'd be haunted for ever. And no woman, however alluring, retained any hold over him once he'd had her.

He came up on one elbow and looked down, saw her eyes flash blue as she looked at him. Her mouth was swollen.

Luca forced down the animalistic urge to take her there and then. He was civilised. He'd spent years convincing people that he wasn't his lush of a mother or his corrupt father.

'No, I didn't.'

He saw her frown slightly. 'Why didn't you...?'

He finished for her, 'Make love to you?'

Serena nodded her head, pulling the sleeping bag

back up over her body. Luca resisted the urge to yank
it back down. *Control.*

His jaw was hard. 'I didn't make love to you, Serena,
because I have no protection with me. And when we do
make love it will be in more comfortable surroundings.'

He sensed her tensing.

'Don't be so sure I want to make love to you, Luca.'

He smiled and felt ruthless. '*Minha beleza*, don't
even *try* to pretend that you would have objected to
making love here and now. I felt your body's response
and it didn't lie. Even if you don't like it.'

She opened her mouth and he reached out and put a
finger to her lips, stopping her words.

'Don't even waste your breath. After that little performance you're mine as surely as if I'd stamped a brand
on your body.'

She smacked his hand away, hard enough to sting.
'Go to hell, Luca.'

Luca curbed the desire to show Serena in a more
subtle way that what he said was true, but it was true
that he didn't have protection, and he knew that if he
touched her again he wouldn't be able to stop himself.

So he lay down and closed his eyes, just saying
darkly, 'Not before I take you with me, *princesa.*'

The fact that he could sense Serena fuming beside
him only made him more determined to shatter her
control again.

She would be his.

The following day Serena was galvanised on her walk—
largely by the depth of her humiliation and her hatred
for Luca. She glared at his back as he strode ahead of

her and mentally envisaged a jaguar springing from the jungle to swallow him whole.

She couldn't get the lurid images out of her head—the way she'd so completely and without hesitation capitulated to Luca's lovemaking. The way he'd played her body like a virtuoso played a violin. The way he'd controlled her reactions while maintaining his own control.

His words mocked her: *'After that little performance you're mine.'* She felt like screaming. Unfortunately it had been no performance—which was galling, considering that for most of her life she'd perfected the performance of a spoilt, reckless heiress.

But on a deeper level what had happened last night with Luca terrified her.

For as long as she could remember there had been a layer between her and the world around her and she was still getting used to that layer being gone. She'd first tasted freedom when her father had disappeared and they'd been left with nothing. It had been too much to deal with, sending her spiralling into a hedonistic frenzy, saved only by her sister taking her to England and to rehab.

Since then she'd learnt to deal with being free; not bearing the constant weight of her father's presence. Her job, becoming independent, was all part of that process. Even if she still harboured deep secrets and a sense of guilt.

But when Luca had been touching her last night—watching her, making her respond to his touch—her sense of freedom had felt very flimsy. Because he'd also been touching a part of her that she hadn't yet given room to really breathe. Her emotions. Her yearning for what her sister had: a life and happiness.

And the fact that Luca had brought that to the surface made her nervous and angry. All she was to him was a conquest. A woman he believed had betrayed him. A woman he wanted to slake his desire with.

A woman he didn't like, even if he ever conceded that she might be innocent.

She'd known that the night they'd met first. He'd had a gleam of disdain in his eyes that he'd barely concealed even as she saw the burn of desire.

And yet, damn him, since she'd walked into his office the other day it was as if everything was brighter, sharper. More intense. *Bastard.*

Serena crashed into Luca's back before she'd even realised she'd been so preoccupied she hadn't noticed he'd stopped. She sprang back, scowling, and then noticed that they were on a kind of bluff, overlooking a huge cleared part of the forest.

To be out from under the slightly oppressive canopy was heady for a moment. Ignoring Luca, Serena studied the view. She could see that far away in the distance the land had been eviscerated. Literally. Huge chunks cut out. No trees. And what looked like huge machines were moving back and forth, sun glinting off steel.

Forgetting that she hated Luca for a moment, because unexpected emotion surged at seeing the forest plundered like this, she asked, a little redundantly, 'That's the mine?'

Luca nodded, his face stern when she sneaked an illicit glance.

'Yes, that's my family's legacy.'

And then he pointed to a dark smudge much closer. 'That's the Iruwaya tribe's village there.'

Serena shaded her eyes until she could make out

what looked like a collection of dusty huts and a clearing. Just then something else caught her eye: a road leading into the village and a bus trundling along merrily, with bags and crates hanging precariously from its roof along with a few live chickens.

It took a few seconds for the scene to compute and for Serena's brain to make sense of it. Slowly she said, 'The village isn't isolated.'

'I never said it was totally isolated.'

The coolness of Luca's tone made Serena step back and look up at him, her blood rapidly rising again. 'So why the hell have we been trekking through a rainforest to get to it?' She added, before he could answer, 'You never said anything about it being optional.'

Luca crossed his arms. 'I didn't offer an option.'

'My God,' Serena breathed. 'You really did do this in a bid to scare me off… I mean, I know you did, but I stupidly thought…'

She trailed off and backed away as the full significance sank in. Her stupid feeling of triumph for putting up the tent last night without help mocked her now. She'd known Luca hated her, that he wanted to punish her…but she hadn't believed for a second that there had been any other way of getting to this village.

All this time he must have been alternating between laughing his head off at her and cursing her for being so determined to stick it out. And then amusing himself by demonstrating how badly she wanted him.

Luca sighed deeply and ran a hand through his hair. 'Serena, this *is* how I'd planned to come to the village, but I'll admit that I thought you would have given up and gone home long before now.'

His words fell on deaf ears. Serena felt exposed, humiliated. She shook her head. 'You're a bastard, Luca Fonseca.'

Terrified of the emotion rising in her chest, she turned and blindly walked away, not taking care to look where she was going.

She'd landed on her hands and knees, the breath knocked out of her, before she realised she'd tripped over something. It also took a moment for her to register that the black ground under her hands was moving.

She sprang back with a small scared yelp just as Luca reached her and hauled her up, turning her to face him.

'Are you okay?'

Still angry with him, Serena broke free. And then she registered a stinging sensation on her arm, and on her thigh. She looked down stupidly, to see her trousers ripped apart from her fall, and vaguely heard Luca curse out loud.

He was pulling her away from where she'd tripped and ripping off her shirt, but Serena was still trying to figure out what had happened—and that was when the pain hit in two places: her arm and her leg.

She cried out in surprise at the shock of how excruciating it was.

Luca was asking urgently, 'Where is it? Where's the pain?'

Struggling, because it was more intense than anything she'd ever experienced, Serena got out thickly, 'My arm…my leg.'

She was barely aware of Luca inspecting her arm, her hands, and then undoing her trousers to pull them down roughly, inspecting her thigh where it was burning. He was brushing something off her and cursing again.

She struggled to recall what she'd seen. Ants. They'd just been ants. It wasn't a snake or a spider.

Luca was doing a thorough inspection of both legs and then moving back up to her arms. In spite of the pain she struggled to get out, 'I'm fine—it's nothing, really.'

But she was feeling nauseous now, with a white-hot sensation blooming outwards from both limbs. She was also starting to shake. Luca pulled her trousers back up. She wasn't even registering embarrassment that he'd all but stripped her.

She tried to take a step, but the pain when she moved almost blinded her. And suddenly she was being lifted into the air against a hard surface. She wanted to tell Luca to put her down but she couldn't seem to formulate the words.

And then the pain took over. There was a sense of time being suspended, loud voices. And then it all went black.

'Serena?'

The voice penetrated the thick warm blanket of darkness that surrounded her. And there was something about the voice that irritated her. She tried to burrow away from it.

'*Serena.*'

'What?' She struggled to open her eyes and winced at the light. Her surroundings registered slowly. A rudimentary hut of some kind. She was lying down on something deliciously soft. And one other thing registered: mercifully...the awful, excruciating pain was gone.

'Welcome back.'

That voice. Deep and infinitely memorable. And not in a good way.

It all came back.

She turned her head to see Luca looking at her with a small smile on his face. *A smile.* He was sitting down near the bed she lay on.

She croaked out, 'What happened?'

His smile faded, and it must have been a trick of the light but she could have sworn he paled slightly. 'You got stung. Badly.'

Serena recalled the ground moving under her hands and shuddered delicately. 'But they were just ants. How could ants do that?'

Luca's mouth twisted. 'They were bullet ants.'

Serena frowned. 'Should that mean anything to me?'

He shook his head. 'Not really, but they deliver a sting that is widely believed to be the most painful on record of any biting insect—like the pain of a bullet. I've been bitten once or twice; I know exactly what it's like.'

Serena felt embarrassed. 'But I passed out like some kind of wimp.'

Luca had a funny look on his face.

'The fact that you were semi-conscious till we reached the village and kept fighting to walk was a testament to your obviously high pain threshold.'

She lifted her arm and looked at it. There was only a very faint redness where she'd been bitten. All that pain and not even a scratch left behind? She almost felt cheated. And then she thought of what he'd said and her arm dropped.

'Wait a second—you carried me all the way here?'

He nodded. There was a scuffling sound from nearby

and thankfully Luca's intense focus moved off her. She looked past him to see some small curious faces peeping around the door. He said something to them and they disappeared, giggling and chattering.

Luca turned back. 'They're fascinated by the golden-haired *gringa* who arrived unconscious into their village a few hours ago.'

Serena was very disorientated by this far less antagonistic Luca. Feeling self-conscious, she struggled to sit up, moving back the covers on the bed.

But Luca rapped out, 'Stay there! You're weak and dehydrated. You're not going anywhere today, or this evening. The women have prepared some food and you need to drink lots of water.'

Luca stood up, and his sheer size made Serena feel dizzy enough to lie down again. As if by magic some smiling women appeared in the doorway, holding various things. Luca ushered them in and said to Serena over their heads, 'I have to go to the mines. I'll be back later. You'll be looked after.'

Weakly, Serena protested, 'But I'm supposed to be taking notes…'

Something flashed in Luca's eyes but he just said, 'Don't worry about that. There'll be time tomorrow, before we have to leave.'

'Before we have to leave.' She felt a lurch in her belly and an awful betraying tingle of anticipation as to what might happen once they did leave this place.

The following morning, early, Luca was trying not to keep staring at Serena, who sat at the end of a long table in the communal eating hut. She was wearing a traditional smock dress, presumably given to her by one of the women to replace her own clothes, and the simple design might have been haute couture, the way she wore it with such effortless grace.

A small toddler, a girl, was sitting on Serena's lap and staring up at her with huge, besotted brown eyes. She'd been crying minutes before, and Serena had bent down to her level and cajoled her to stop crying, lifting her up and settling her as easily as if she was her mother.

Now she was eating her breakfast—a manioc-based broth—for all the world acting as if it was the finest caviar, giving the little girl morsels in between her own mouthfuls. She couldn't have looked more innocent and pure if she'd tried, tugging remorselessly on his conscience.

A mixture of rage and sexual frustration made Luca's whole body tight. The remnants of the panic he'd felt the previous day when she'd been so limp in his arms after being stung still clung to him. She'd been brave. Even though he knew he was being completely irrational, he couldn't stop lambasting her inwardly for not behaving as he expected her to.

Their eyes met and caught at that moment and he saw her cheeks flush. With desire? Or anger? Or a mixture of both like him? Suddenly her significance wasn't important any more—who she was, what she'd done. Or not done. He wanted her, and she would pay for throwing his life out of whack not once but twice.

Resolve filling his body, he stood up and said curtly, 'We're leaving for the mines in ten minutes.'

He didn't like the way he noticed how her arm tightened around the small girl almost protectively, or how seeing a child on her lap made him feel. All sorts of things he'd never imagined feeling in his life—ever.

Her chin tipped up. 'I'll be ready.'

Luca left before he did something stupid, like take up his phone and ask for the helicopter to come early so that he could haul her back to Rio and douse this fire in his blood as soon as possible.

CHAPTER SIX

A FEW HOURS later Serena was back in her own clothes, now clean, and sitting cross-legged beside Luca in the hut of the tribal elders. She was still smarting from the intensity of his regard that morning at breakfast. As if he'd been accusing her of something. Her suspicions had been reinforced when he'd said, with a definitely accusatory tone, on their journey to the mines, 'You were good with that little girl earlier.'

Serena had swallowed back the tart urge to apologise and explained, 'I have a nephew just a little bit older. We're very close.'

She hadn't liked being reminded of that vulnerability—that from the moment she'd held Siena's son, Spiro, he and Serena had forged an indelible bond and her biological clock had started ticking loudly.

For someone who had never seen the remotest possibility of such a domestic idyll in her life, she was still surprised at how much she craved it.

And she hated it that she'd barely slept a wink in the hut because she'd missed knowing Luca's solid bulk was just inches away. She dragged her attention back to what she was meant to be focusing on: writing notes as fast as Luca translated what he wanted taken down.

They'd spent the morning at the mines and she'd seen how diplomatic he had to be, trying to assuage the fears of the miners about losing their jobs, while attempting to drag the mine and its administration into the twenty-first century and minimise further damage to the land. It was a very fine balancing act.

When he was being diplomatic and charming he was truly devastating. It gave Serena a very strong sense of just how seductive he could be if...if he actually liked her. The thought of that made her belly swoop alarmingly.

He turned to her now. 'Did you get that?'

She looked at the notes quickly. 'About coming up with ideas to actively promote and nurture growth in the local economy?'

He nodded. But before he turned back to the tribal leader Serena followed an impulse and touched his arm. He frowned at her, and she smiled hesitantly at the man Luca was talking to before saying, 'Could I make a suggestion?'

He drew back a few inches and looked at her. His entire stance was saying, *You?*

Serena fought off the urge to hit him and gritted her teeth. 'Those smock dresses that the women make—I haven't seen them anywhere else. Also, the little carvings that the children have been doing... I know that this village is twinned with another one, and they have monthly fair days when they barter goods and crops and utilise their skills and learn from each other...but what about opening it up a bit—say, having a space in Rio, or Manaus, a charity shop that sells the things they make here. And in the other village. A niche market, with the money coming back directly to the people.'

'That's hardly a novel idea,' Luca said coolly.

Serena refused to be intimidated or feel silly. 'Well, if it's not a new concept why hasn't one of these shops been mentioned anywhere in your literature about the charity? I'm not talking about some rustic charity shop. I'm talking about a high-end finish that'll draw in discerning tourists and buyers. Something that'll inspire them to help conserve the rainforest.'

Luca said nothing for a long moment, and then he turned back to the chief and spoke to him rapidly. The man's old, lined face lit up and he smiled broadly, nodding effusively.

Luca looked back to Serena, a conciliatory gleam in his eyes. 'I'll look into it back in Rio.'

The breath she hadn't even been aware of holding left her chest and she had to concentrate when the conversation started again. Finally, when Luca and the chief had spoken for an hour or so, they got up to leave. The old man darted forward with surprising agility to take Serena's hand in his and pump it up and down vigorously. She smiled at his effervescence.

Following Luca out into the slightly less intense late-afternoon heat, she could see a Jeep approach in the distance.

Luca looked at his watch. 'That'll be our lift to the airfield. We need to pack our stuff up.'

He looked at her and must have seen something that Serena had failed to disguise in time.

His eyes glinted with something indefinable. 'I thought you'd welcome the prospect of civilisation again?'

'I do,' Serena said quickly, avoiding his look. But the truth was that she didn't…exactly. Their couple of days in the rainforest…the otherworldly pace of life in the village…it had soothed something inside her. And she realised that she would miss it.

Afraid Luca might see that, she folded her arms and said, 'Are you going to give me a chance?' And then quickly, before he could interject, 'I think I deserve it. I don't want to go home yet.'

Luca looked at her. She could see the Jeep coming closer, stopping. She held her breath. His gaze narrowed on her and became…*hot.* Instantly Serena felt something spike. Anticipation.

He came closer, blocking out the Jeep arriving, the village behind him.

'I've no intention of letting you go home.'

Serena's arms clenched tighter. She didn't like the way her body reacted to that implacable statement and what it might mean. 'You're giving me a trial period?'

Luca smiled, and it made Serena's brain fuzzy.

'Something like that. I told you I wanted you, Serena. And I do. In my bed.'

Anger spiked at his arrogant tone, even as her pulse leapt treacherously. 'I'm not interested in becoming your next mistress, Fonseca. I'm interested in working.'

Luca's eyes flashed at her use of 'Fonseca'. 'I'll give you a two-week trial. Two weeks of working in the charity by day and two weeks in my bed by night.'

Serena unclenched her arms, her hands in fists by her sides, hating the betraying sizzle in her blood. Had she no self-respect?

'That's blackmail.'

Luca shrugged, supremely unconcerned. 'Call it what you want. That's the only way you'll get your trial.'

Serena swallowed a caustic rush of tangled emotions

along with the betraying hum of desire. 'And what about your precious reputation? If people see us together? What then?'

Luca moved closer. Serena's words struck him somewhere deep inside. What *was* he doing? he asked himself. All he knew was that the things that had been of supreme importance to him for a long time no longer seemed as important. There was only here and now and this woman. And *heat*. And need.

Yet he wasn't losing sight of what had driven him for all these years completely. He was cynical enough to recognise an opportunity when it arose. Having Serena on his arm would mean news, and news would mean focus on the things close to his heart. Like his foundation.

He said now, 'I have every intention of people seeing us together. You see, I've realised that seven years is like seven lifetimes in the media world. You're old news. And if anyone does make something of it I'm quite happy for you to be seen by my side as someone intent on making up for her debauched past by doing charity work. Everyone loves a redemption story, after all. And in the meantime I get what I want—which is *you*. You owe me, Serena. You don't think I'm going to give you a two-week trial without recompense, do you?'

Serena just looked at him. She was too stunned to say anything. What Luca had said was so...*cold*. And yet all she could feel was *hot*. She should be slapping him across the face and taking a bus back to Manaus and the next flight home. Maybe that was what he was doing? Calling her bluff. Goading her. She couldn't imagine that he didn't have a string of willing mistresses back in Rio.

But that only made something very dark rise up: jealousy.

'We leave in fifteen minutes.'

With that he turned and strode away, as if he hadn't just detonated a bomb between them. She watched him incredulously, and then stalked to the small hut.

As she packed up her small backpack a few minutes later she alternated between the longing to to find Luca and deliver that slap to his face which he so deserved and pausing to remember how it had felt when he'd kissed her and touched her the other night.

She'd never really enjoyed sex; it had been another route to oblivion which had invariably ended in disappointment and an excoriating sense of self-disgust.

But Luca… It was as if he was able to see right through to her deepest self, to the part of her that was still innocent, untainted by what she'd seen and experienced as a child…

'Ms DePiero?'

Serena whirled around to see a young man in the doorway of the hut.

'Senhor Fonseca is waiting for you at the Jeep.'

Serena muttered something about coming and watched the man walk away. Something inside her solidified. She could leave and go home, lose any chance of a job with the charity and start all over again. Concede defeat. Or…if she was going to admit to herself that she wanted Luca too…she could be as strategic as him.

But if she was going to stay and submit to his arrogant demands then it would be on *her* terms, and she would gain from it too.

Luca sent a wary glance to Serena, who was sitting on the other side of the plane. She was looking out of the window, so he couldn't see her expression, but he would guess that it was as stony as it had been when she'd got into the Jeep and on the silent journey to the private airfield near the airport.

He wasn't flying the plane this time. Ostensibly so he could catch up on work, but for possibly the first time in his life he couldn't focus on it.

All he could focus on was Serena, and the tense lines of her slim body, and wonder what that stony silence meant. He knew he deserved it. He was surprised she hadn't slapped him back at the village. He'd seen the moment in her expression when she'd wanted to.

He'd never behaved so autocratically with a woman in his life. If he wanted a woman he seduced her and took her to bed, and they were never under the impression that he was in the market for more than that.

But this was Serena DePiero. From the first moment he'd ever seen her he'd been tangled up into knots. The last few days had shown him a vastly different woman from the one he'd met before...and yet hadn't he seen something of this woman in her eyes that night in the club? He didn't like to admit that he *had* seen that moment of vulnerability.

His conscience pricked him. *He'd all but black-mailed her.* He wasn't so deluded that he couldn't acknowledge uncomfortably that it had been a crass attempt on his behalf to get her where he wanted her without having to let her know how badly he needed to sate this hunger inside him.

He opened his mouth to speak to her just as she turned her head to look at him and those searing blue eyes robbed him of speech. She looked determined.

'I've been thinking about your...proposal.'

Luca's conscience hit him again. He winced inwardly. Never had he imagined that she would be so diplomatic when he'd been such a bastard. 'Serena—'

She held up a hand. 'No, let me speak.'

He closed his mouth and didn't like the flutter of panic at the thought that he might just have completely mismanaged this. She could leave now and he'd never see her again.

'If I agree to stay and do this trial for two weeks... If I do well—prove that I'm capable...and...' She stopped, a dark flush staining her cheeks before she continued. 'If I agree to what you said...then I want you to assure me that you'll give me a job—whether it's here or back in Athens. A proper contracted, paying job for the charity.'

The relief that flowed through Luca was unsettling and heady. His conscience still struck him, but he was too distracted to deal with it.

He held out a hand towards Serena and growled, 'Come here.'

The flush on her cheeks got pinker. 'Luca—'

'Come here and I'll tell you.'

He saw her bite her lip, the dart of her pink tongue. After a few seconds her hands went to her belt and she undid it and pushed herself up and out of her seat. As soon as she was within touching distance Luca had closed a hand around her wrist and tugged her so that she fell onto his lap with a soft *ooph*.

'Luca, what are you—?'

He couldn't help himself. He covered her mouth with his and stopped her words. A very dangerous kind of relief flowed through him. She would be his. She wasn't leaving. Her arms crept around his neck after a moment of resistance. Her mouth softened under his. And when he swept his tongue along hers, and she sighed, he could have howled with triumph.

Before he lost it completely he drew back, his breathing laboured. He touched a hand to her jaw, cupping it, running a finger along its delicate line. He looked into her eyes and said, 'Yes, I'll give you a job.'

He could feel Serena's breath making her chest shudder against him. The pressure in his groin intensified.

'I want a signed agreement, Luca, that you'll keep your word.'

Indignation made anger flare. 'You don't trust me?' It had all been about him not trusting *her*. Luca had never considered her not trusting *him*, and it didn't sit well.

Serena's lush mouth compressed. She didn't answer directly, she said, 'A promise on paper, Luca, or I'll leave as soon as we touch down.'

Any feeling of triumph or any sense of control slipped out of Luca's grasp. His hands were around Serena's hips, holding her to him, and as much as he wanted to push her back, tell her that no woman dictated to him…he couldn't. The taste of her was on his tongue and, dammit, it wasn't enough. Not yet.

So he finally bit out, 'Fine.'

Serena took in the frankly mind-boggling three-hundred-and-sixty-degree view of Rio de Janeiro outside the glass walls of the penthouse apartment. It was at the top of the building she'd come to that first day.

She turned to face Luca. 'This is your apartment?'

He was watching her intently and inclined his head. 'Yes, but I only use it if I'm working late, or for entertaining clients after meetings.'

Or for entertaining mistresses?

Suddenly she didn't feel half as sure as she had on the plane, when Luca had pulled her into his lap to kiss her. Now her doubts and insecurities were back. Luca affected her...too much.

She crossed her arms. 'I can't stay here. It's inappropriate.'

Luca stifled an inelegant snort. 'This from the woman who was photographed at her debs in an exclusive Paris hotel in a bathtub full of champagne while dressed in a priceless gown?'

Serena flushed, recalling her father's malevolent smile and even more malevolent tone of voice: *'Good girl. We wouldn't want people to think you're becoming boring, now, would we?'*

Serena chose to ignore Luca's comment. 'What about the apartment I was meant to stay in? The one for staff?'

'It's no longer available; someone else took your place there.'

'Well, that's hardly my fault, is it?' she retorted hotly.

Luca's jaw firmed. 'It's either here, Serena, or if you insist, the charity will be put to the expense of finding you somewhere else.'

'No!' she shot out, aghast. 'But it's just—'

He cut in coolly. 'You're staying here. I'm sure you can put up with it for two weeks.'

This was what she was afraid of. He made her emotions and blood pressure see-saw out of control.

Luca looked at Serena and narrowed his gaze. She was skittish, nervy. A million miles from the woman who had melted in his arms just a short time before.

'Serena, what is it?'

She was angry, her cheeks growing pink. 'I've agreed

to sleep with you to get a job—how do you think that makes me feel?'

Luca's conscience pricked but he pointed out, 'You're not sleeping with me yet.'

She went redder.

Luca felt something give inside him and ran a hand through his hair impatiently. 'Look, I behaved like a boor earlier. The very least you deserve is a trial period. I would have given it to you anyway.'

She looked at him, surprised, and it affected him more than he'd like to admit.

'You would? And what about a job?'

Luca schooled his features. 'That depends on your trial period—as it would for anyone else.'

He moved closer then, and put his hands on her upper arms. 'And you are *not* sleeping with me to get a job. You're sleeping with me because it's what you want. What we *both* want.'

She just looked at him, and something desperate rose inside Luca. He ground out, 'The door is behind me, Serena. You can walk out right now if that's what you want and you'll still get your trial.'

For an infinitesimal moment she said nothing, and he was reminded of telling her where the door was before, willing her to use it. Now he'd launch an army if she tried to leave. He had to consciously stop his hands from gripping her arms tight, as if he could restrain her from walking out. He could see her throat work as she swallowed. Her eyes were wide, pupils as black as night.

She opened her mouth and he kept his eyes off the seductive temptation of those soft lips. He needed to hear this too badly. Needed her to stay.

'Serena…'

Her tongue moistened those lips. Luca's pulse jumped.

Her voice was husky. 'I just want a chance.'

The tension in Luca's body spiked. *Damn her.* 'And? What else?'

She turned her head away and bitterness laced her voice. 'You know I want you. In the tent…you made me show you. You humiliated me.'

Luca's chest was tight enough to hurt. An alien sensation. He cursed softly and felt as if some layer of himself was being stripped away when he admitted, 'Do you know how hard it was for me to stop myself from taking you that night?'

Those blue eyes locked with his. She whispered, 'You made me feel as if you just wanted to prove your dominance over me.'

Luca tipped her chin up with a finger and felt her jaw clench. He smiled, and it was wry. 'You credit me with far too much forethought. I needed to hear you say it…that you wanted me. You made *me* feel that much out of control.'

Instantly something flashed in those piercing eyes— something that made some of Luca's tightness ease.

'You're so in control. It's almost scary.'

Now Luca was the one to grit his jaw as he recognised that no one had ever said that to him before—certainly not a woman. Serena's gaze seemed to see right through him to where he stood as a small boy, witnessing the awesome power parents had to rip your life apart. He knew his desire for control and respectability stemmed from that chaotic, messy, tumultuous moment. And here he was, skating far too close to the edges of losing it all again. And yet…he couldn't walk away.

He said, with quiet conviction, 'If I was to kiss you right now you'd see how thin the veneer of my control is, believe me.'

Something hot flared in the bright blue depths and he stifled a groan of pure need. But he would not take her now, like this, after trekking in a jungle for days, when they were both dizzy with fatigue.

It was the hardest thing in the world, but he let her go and stepped back. 'I have work to catch up on—some conference calls to make. And I'm sure you'll appreciate a night in a real bed again. My assistant will be here in the morning to take you down to the charity offices where you'll be working. And tomorrow evening I'm taking you to a charity function.'

Serena's heart palpitated with a mixture of relief and disappointment. So he wasn't staying tonight? And then shame lanced her that she hadn't been strong enough just to walk away. That a part of her wanted to explore what this man was offering, almost more than she wanted to prove herself or ensure her independence.

The last three and a half years had been all about finding and nurturing an inner strength she'd never known she had. But Luca made her feel weak, and it scared her. But not enough to turn away from him. Damn him.

'Okay.'

Luca said nothing for a long moment and then he said quietly, '*Boa noite,* Serena. *Até amanha.*'

Till tomorrow.

He turned and walked away and the slick, modern apartment was immediately cavernous without him. They'd only spent four days together but it felt like a lifetime. Serena battled the urge to flee, once again questioning her rationale... But her decision to stay had nothing to do with being rational. That had fled out of the window as soon as Luca had pulled her onto his lap on the plane and kissed her witless.

Doubts and fears melted away. She wasn't going anywhere. She couldn't.

As soon as that registered in her body fatigue and exhaustion hit her like a freight train. Along with the realisation that she had hot water at her disposal and could finally wash.

Pushing all thoughts of Luca and what the immediate future held out of her head, she unpacked, took the longest and most delicious shower she'd ever had in her life, fell face-down onto an indescribably soft bed, and sank into oblivion.

Luca stood at the window of his office a floor below the apartment. Rio was a carpet of twinkling golden lights as far as the eye could see. He spoke into the mobile he held to his ear.

His voice was tight. 'Let's just say that I have my doubts about whether she did it or not, and I'd appreciate your help in finding out.' There was a pause, and then Luca said curtly, 'Look, Max, if it's too much trouble—' He sighed. 'Okay, yes. And, thanks, I appreciate it.'

Luca cut the connection and threw his phone down on the table behind him. It bounced off and hit the carpeted floor. He ignored it and turned back to the view. Any conversation with his brother drove his blood pressure skywards. He knew that Max didn't blame Luca specifically for the fact that they'd been split up the way they had between their parents...but guilt festered inside Luca even now. He was the elder twin and he'd always felt that responsibility keenly.

Pushing thoughts of his brother aside, Luca hated to admit it, but he felt altered in some way. As if some alchemy had taken place in his head and body since he'd stood looking at this view the last time—just before Serena had arrived almost a week ago.

He scowled at his fanciful thoughts. There was no alchemy. It was physical attraction, pure and simple. It had been between them from the moment their eyes had first locked. And now he was going to sate it. That was all.

The fact that he was prepared to allow Serena De-Piero to sign an agreement which would potentially offer her employment with his company for the fore-seeable future, *and* to be seen with her in public, were things that he pushed to the deepest recesses of his mind.

He focused instead on the increasing anticipation in his blood and his body at the knowledge that soon this ever-present hunger would be assuaged.

CHAPTER SEVEN

THE FOLLOWING EVENING Serena waited on the outdoor terrace that wrapped around the entire apartment, a ball of nerves in her gut. The fact that Luca had said he was taking her to a charity function had been conveniently forgotten when she'd succumbed to exhaustion the previous evening—and in the whirlwind of the day she'd just had.

She'd woken early and had some breakfast just before his sleek assistant Laura had arrived, cracking a minute smile for once. She'd handed Serena a sheaf of papers and hot embarrassment had risen up when she'd seen it was the contract assuring her of work if she completed her trial period successfully. The contract she'd demanded.

To her relief there was no mention of the more personal side of their agreement. Luca's cool efficiency was scary.

After she'd signed, Laura had taken her down to the first floor, where the offices for the charity were based, and introduced her to the staff. Serena had spent such a pleasant day with the friendly Brazilians, who had been so nice and patient with her rudimentary Portuguese that she'd almost fooled herself into forgetting what else awaited her.

But she couldn't ignore it any longer. Not when she'd returned to the apartment to find a stylist and a troupe of hair and make-up people waiting to transform her for Luca's pleasure. Or *delectation* might be a better word. She felt like something that should be on display.

An entire wardrobe of designer clothes seemed to have materialised by magic during the day, and this whole process brought back so many memories of her old life—when her father had insisted on making sure his daughters had the most desirable clothes…for the maximum effect.

The thought of the evening ahead made her go clammy. Right now, weakly, she'd take a jungle full of scorpions, snakes, bullet ants and even an angry Luca Fonseca over the social jungle she was about to walk into.

And then she drew herself up tall. She was better than this. Was she forgetting what she'd survived in the past few years? The intense personal scrutiny and soul-searching? The constant invasion of her privacy as she'd faced her demons in front of strangers? And not only that—she'd survived the jungle with Luca, who'd been waiting for her to falter at every step.

Although right now that didn't feel so much of a triumph as a test of endurance that she was still undergoing. They'd exchanged the wild jungle for the so-called civilised jungle. And this time the stakes were so much higher.

At that moment the little hairs all over her body stood up a nano-second before she heard a noise behind her. She had no time to keep obsessing over whether or not she'd picked out the right dress. Squaring her shoulders, and drawing on the kind of reserves that she hadn't had to call on in years, Serena turned around.

For a second she could only blink to make sure she wasn't dreaming. Her ability to breathe was severely compromised. Memories of Luca seven years ago slammed into her like a punch to the gut. Except this Luca was infinitely harder, more gorgeous.

'You've shaved...' Serena commented faintly. But those words couldn't do justice to the man in front of her, dressed in a classic tuxedo, his hard jaw revealed in all its obduracy, the sensual lines of his mouth even more defined.

His thick dark hair was shorter too, and Serena felt an irrational spurt of jealousy for whoever had had his or her hands on his head.

She was too enflamed and stunned by this vision of Luca to notice that his gaze had narrowed on her and a flush had made his cheeks darken.

'You look...incredible.'

Luca's eyes felt seared, right through to the back. She was a sleek, beautiful goddess. All he could see at first was bare skin, arms and shoulders. And acres of red silk and gold, sparkling with inlaid jewels. A deep V drew his eye effortlessly to luscious curves. There was some embellishment on the shoulders and then the dress fell in a swathe of silk and lace from her waist to the floor. He could see the hint of one pale thigh peeping out from the luxurious folds and had to grit his jaw to stop his body from exploding.

She'd pinned her hair back into a low bun at the base of her neck. It should have made the outfit look more demure than if her hair had been around her shoulders in a silken white-golden tumble, but it didn't. It seemed to heighten the provocation of the dress.

Luca registered then that she looked uncomfortable.

Shifting minutely, those long fingers were fluttering near the V of the dress, as if to try and cover it up. The woman Luca had seen in Florence had been wearing a fraction of this much material and revelling in it.

She was avoiding his eye, and that made Luca move closer. She looked up and his pulse fired. He came close enough to smell her clean, fresh scent. Suddenly it felt as if he hadn't seen her in a month, when it had been just a day. A day in which he'd had to restrain himself from going down to the charity offices.

Danger.

He ignored it.

He might have expected her scent to be overpowering, overtly sensual, but it was infinitely more subtle.

Familiar irritation that she was proving to be more difficult to grasp than quicksilver made him say brusquely, 'What's wrong? The dress? You don't like it?'

She looked up at him and need gripped Luca so fiercely that his whole body tensed. But something very cynical followed. He'd had an entire wardrobe of clothes delivered to the apartment—and she wasn't happy?

Her eyes flashed. 'No, it's not the dress.' Her voice turned husky. 'The dress is beautiful. But what were you thinking, sending all those clothes? I'm not your mistress, and I don't want to be treated like one.'

Surprise lanced him, but he recovered quickly. 'I thought you'd appreciate being prepared for a public event.'

Serena looked down and muttered, 'You mean public humiliation.'

Something shifted in Luca's chest. He tipped up her chin, more concerned than he liked to admit by her uneasiness. Colour stained her pale cheeks and Luca almost gave in to the beast inside him. *Almost*. With a supreme effort he willed it down. 'What I said before… about exposing you to public scrutiny…that won't happen, Serena. I won't let it.'

Her eyes were wide. *Wounded*? Her mouth thinned. 'Isn't that part of the plan, though? A little revenge?'

Luca winced inwardly. What did this woman do to him? She called to his most base instincts and he could be as cruel as his father ever had been. Shame washed through him.

He shook his head, something fierce erupting inside him. 'I'm taking you out because I want to be seen with you, Serena.'

As he said it he realised it was true. He genuinely wanted this. To have her on his arm. And it had very little to do with wanting to punish her. At the thought of adverse public reaction a protective instinct nearly bowled him over with its force.

Before he could lose his footing completely, he took her by the hand and said gruffly, 'We should leave or we'll be late.'

In the lift something caught his eye, and he looked down to see Serena's other hand clutching a small bag which matched her dress. Her knuckles were white, and when his gaze travelled up he could see the tension in her body and jaw.

The lift jerked softly to a halt and almost against his will Luca found his hand going to the small of Serena's back to touch her. The minute his hand came into contact with the bare, warm, silky skin left exposed by the backless design she tensed more.

He frowned as something had dawned on him. 'Are you…*nervous*?'

Serena's eyes flashed with some indefinable emotion and she quickly stepped out of the open doors of the elevator, away from his touch, avoiding his narrowed gaze.

'Don't be ridiculous. It's just been a while since I've gone to anything like this, that's all.'

Luca sensed that there was a lot more to it than that, but he gestured for her to precede him out of the building, realising too late what awaited them outside when a veritable explosion of light seemed to go off in their faces. Without even realising what he was doing he put his arm around Serena and curved her into his body, one hand up to cover her face, as they walked quickly to his car, where a security guard held the passenger door open.

In the car, Serena's heart was pumping so hard she felt light-headed. The shock of that wall of paparazzi when she hadn't seen it in so long was overwhelming. And she couldn't help the fierce pain of betrayal. Everything Luca had just said was lies...and she hated that she wouldn't have expected it of him.

She was a sap. Of *course* he was intent on—

Her hand was taken in a firm grip. She clenched her jaw and looked at Luca in the driver's seat. His face was dark...*with anger*?

'Serena, I had nothing to do with that. They must have been tipped off.'

He looked so grim and affronted that Serena felt something melt inside her. Felt a wish to believe him.

'It won't happen again.'

She took her hand from Luca's and forced a smile. 'Don't worry about it.'

The imprint of Luca's body where he'd held her so close was still making her treacherous skin tingle all over. The way he'd drawn her into him so protectively had unsettled her. She'd felt unprotected for so long that it was an alien sensation. Maybe he *hadn't* planned it. She recalled him biting off a curse now, as if he'd been as surprised as her...

Once they'd left the paparazzi behind she pushed a button to lower her window, relishing the warm evening Rio breeze and the tang of the sea.

'Are you okay?'

Serena nodded. 'Fine—just needed some air.'

The setting sun was bathing the sky in a pink glow, and from somewhere distant Serena could hear cheers and clapping.

She looked at Luca. 'What's that?'

Luca's mouth twitched. 'Every evening sunset-worshippers applaud another stunning sunset from the beaches.'

Serena couldn't take her eyes off the curve of Luca's mouth. 'I love that idea,' she breathed. 'I'd like to see the sunset.'

She quickly looked away again, in case that dark navy gaze met hers when she felt far too exposed. Her cheeks were still hot from that moment when she'd been captivated by the way he filled out his suit so effortlessly. The obviously bespoke material did little to disguise his sheer power, flowing lovingly over defined muscles.

'Where do you live when you don't stay at the apartment?' Serena blurted out the first thing she could think of to try and take her mind off Luca's physicality.

He glanced at her, his hands strong on the wheel of the car.

'I have a house in Alto Gavea—it's a district in the Tijuca Forest, north of the lake…'

She sneaked a look. 'Is it your family home? Where you grew up?'

He shook his head abruptly, and when he answered his voice was tight. 'No, we lived out in the suburbs. My parents wouldn't have approved of living so near to the beaches and *favelas*.'

Serena thought of what he'd told her about his parents so far and asked, 'You weren't close to them?'

His mouth twisted. 'No. They split up when we were six, and my mother moved back to her native Italy.'

Serena had forgotten about that Italian connection. 'You said *we*… Do you have brothers and sisters?'

She could sense his reluctance to answer, but they weren't going anywhere fast in the evening traffic. Luca sighed. 'Yes, I have a twin brother.'

Serena's eyes widened. 'Wow—a twin? That's pretty amazing.' Her mind boggled slightly at the thought of *two* Lucas.

He slid her a mocking look and said, 'We're non-identical. He lives in Italy; he moved there with our mother after the divorce.'

Serena processed this and turned in her seat to face him. 'Wait…you mean you were split up?'

The thought of anyone splitting her and Siena up at that young age made her go cold. Siena had been the only anchor in her crazy world.

Luca faced forward, his voice emotionless. 'Yes, my parents decided that each would take one of us. My mother chose me to go to Italy with her, but when my brother got upset she swapped us and took him instead.'

Serena gasped as that scenario sank in. 'But that's…
horrific. And your father just let her?'

Luca looked at her, face hard. 'He didn't care which
son he got as long as he got one of us to be his heir.'

Serena knew what it was to grow up under a cruel
tyrant, but this shocked even her. 'And are you close
now? You and your brother?'

Luca shrugged minutely. 'Not particularly. But he
was the one who bailed me out of jail, and he was the
one who arranged for the best legal defence to get me
out of Florence and back to Rio, avoiding a lengthy
trial and jail time.'

His expression hardened to something infinitely
cynical.

'A hefty donation towards "the preservation of
Florence" was all it took to get the trial mysteriously
dismissed. That money undoubtedly went to corrupt
officials—one of whom was probably your father—
but I was damned if I was going to hang for a crime I
wasn't even responsible for. But they wouldn't clear me
completely, so every time I fly to Europe now I come
under the radar of Europe's law enforcement agencies.'

Serena felt cold. She turned back to the front, staring unseeingly out of the window, knowing it was futile
to say anything. She'd protested her innocence till she
was blue in the face, but Luca was right—his association with her *had* made things worse for him.

They were turning into a vast tree-lined driveway
now, which led up to a glittering colonial-style building. When Luca pulled up, and a valet parker waited
for him to get out, Serena took several deep breaths to
calm her frayed nerves.

Luca surprised her by not getting out straight away.

He turned to her. 'I'm not interested in the past any more, Serena. I'm interested in the here and now.'

Serena swallowed. Something fragile seemed to shimmer between them…tantalising. And then he got out of the car and she sucked in another shaky breath.

He came around and opened her door, extended a hand to help her out. She took it, and when his gaze tracked down her body and lingered on her breasts a pulse throbbed between her legs.

He tucked her arm into his as they moved forward and joined similarly dressed couples entering a glittering doorway lit by hundreds of small lights. It was a scene Serena had seen a million times before, but never heightened like this. Never *romantic*.

She asked herself as Luca led her inside, greeting someone in Portuguese, if they really could let the past go. Or was that just what Luca was willing to say so that he could bed her and then walk away, with all that resentment still simmering under the surface?

'Do you think you could crack a smile and not look as if you're about to be subjected to torture?'

Serena glanced at Luca, who had a fixed social smile on his face. She sent up silent thanks that he couldn't read her thoughts and said sweetly. 'But this *is* torture.'

Something flared in his eyes—surprise?—and then he said, 'Torture it may well be, but a few hours of social torture is worth it if it means that a *favela* gets a new free school staffed by qualified teachers.'

Serena felt immediately chastened. 'Is that what this evening's ball is in aid of?'

Luca looked at her assessingly. 'Among some other causes. The global communities charity too.'

Serena thought of that sweet little girl in the village—a million miles away from here…and yet *not*.

'I'm sorry,' she said huskily. 'You're right—it *is* worth it.'

Serena missed Luca's speculative look because a waiter was interrupting them with a tray of champagne. Luca took a glass and looked at her when she didn't.

She shook her head quickly and said to the waiter, 'Do you have some sparkling water, please?'

The waiter rushed off and Luca frowned slightly. 'You really don't drink any more?'

Serena's belly clenched. 'No, I really don't.' She made a face. 'I never liked the taste of alcohol anyway. It was more for the effect it had on me.'

'What was that?'

She looked at him. 'Numbing.'

The moment stretched between them…taut. And then the attentive waiter returned with a glass of water on a tray for Serena. She took it gratefully. Luca was getting too close to that dark place inside her.

To her relief someone came up then, and took his attention, but just as Serena felt hopeful that he might forget about her she felt her heart sink and jump in equal measure when she felt him reach for her hand and tug her with him, introducing her to the man.

Luca was finding it hard to concentrate on the conversation around him when he usually had no problem. Even if he *was* with a woman. He was aware of every tiny movement Serena made in that dress, and acutely aware of the attention she was attracting.

He was also aware that she seemed ill at ease. He'd expected her to come back into this kind of environment and take to it like the proverbial duck to water, but when they'd first come in she'd looked *pained*. It was just like in the jungle, when she'd proved him resoundingly wrong in his expectations of her.

Now her head was bent towards one of the executive team who managed his charities abroad, and they were engaged in an earnest conversation when Luca would have fully expected Serena to look bored out of her brains.

At that moment her head tipped back and she laughed at something the other woman had said. Luca couldn't breathe, and the conversation stopped around them as she unwittingly drew everyone's eye. She literally... *sparkled*, her face transformed by her wide smile. She was undeniably beautiful...and Luca realised he'd never seen true beauty till that moment.

His chest felt tight as he had a vision of what he'd subjected her to: dragging her into the jungle on a forced trek. She'd endured one of the most painful insect bites in the world. She'd stayed in a rustic village in the depths of the Amazon without blinking. She'd endeared herself to the tribespeople without even trying. It had taken him *years* to be accepted and respected.

And the miners—some of the hardest men in Brazil—weathered and rough as they came—they'd practically been doffing their caps when Serena had appeared with him, as if she was royalty.

Luca could see the crowd moving towards the ballroom and took Serena's hand in his. She looked at him with that smile still playing about her mouth and a sense of yearning stronger than anything he'd ever felt kicked him in the solar plexus. A yearning to be the cause of such a smile.

As if she was reading his mind her smile faded on cue.

'Come on—let's dance,' Luca growled, feeling unconstructed. Raw.

He tugged Serena in his wake before he remembered that he didn't even *like* dancing, but right now he needed to feel her body pressed against his or he might go crazy.

When they reached the edge of the dimly lit dance floor Luca turned and pulled her with him, facing her. The light highlighted her stunning bone structure. That effortlessly classic beauty.

Unbidden, he heard himself articulate the question resounding in his head. 'Who *are* you?'

She swallowed. 'You know who I am.'

'Do I really?' he asked, almost angry now. 'Or is this all some grand charade for the benefit of your family, so you can go back to doing what you love best—being a wild society princess?'

Serena went pale and pulled free of Luca's embrace, saying angrily, 'I've told you about me but you still don't have the first clue, Luca. And as for what I love best? You'll never know.'

She turned and was walking away, disappearing into the vast lobby, before Luca realised that he was struck dumb and immobile because no woman had ever walked away from him before.

Cursing under his breath, he followed her, but when he got to the lobby there was no sign of a distinctive red dress or a white-blonde head. The way she'd stood out in the crowd mocked him now. His gut clenched with panic.

He got to the open doors, where people were still arriving. He spotted the valet who had taken his car and accosted him, asking curtly, 'The woman I came with—have you seen her?'

The valet gulped, visibly intimidated by Luca. 'Yes. Sir. I just saw her into a taxi that had dropped off some guests.'

Luca swore so volubly that the valet's ears went red. He stammered, 'Do—do you want your car?'

Luca just looked at him expressively and the young man scurried off.

They were on a hill overlooking the city. Luca looked out onto the benignly twinkling lights of Rio and the panic intensified. He recalled Serena saying she wanted to see the sunset... Would she have gone to the beach? At this time of night?

Panic turned to fear. He took out his phone and made a call to Serena's mobile but it was switched off. Rio was a majestic city, but at night certain areas were some of the most dangerous on earth. Where the *hell* had she gone?

Serena stalked into the apartment and the door slammed behind her with a gratifyingly loud bang. She was still shaking with anger, and her emotions were bubbling far too close to the surface for comfort.

She kicked off her shoes and made her way out to the terrace, taking deep breaths. Damn Luca Fonseca. It shouldn't matter what he thought of her...but after everything they'd been through she'd foolishly assumed that he'd come to see that she *was* different.

This was the real her. A woman who wanted to work and do something worthwhile, and never, ever insulate herself against life again. The girl and the young woman she'd been had been born out of the twisted machinations of her father.

Her hands wrapped around the railing. Self-disgust rose up inside her. To think that she was willing to go to bed with a man who thought so little of her. Where was the precious self-esteem she'd painstakingly built up again?

She knew where... It had all dissolved in a puddle of heat as soon as Luca came within feet of her. And yet she knew that wasn't entirely fair—he'd treated her as his exact equal in the jungle, and earlier, in the charity offices, she'd been surprised to find that he'd already put in motion discussions on her idea for a high-end tourist shop showcasing products from the villages and credited her with the plan.

She heard a sound behind her and tensed. Panic washed through her. She wasn't ready to deal with Luca yet. But reluctantly she turned around to see him advancing on her, his face like thunder, as long fingers pulled at his bow-tie.

She still got a jolt of sensation to see him clean-shaven. It should have made him look more urbane. It didn't.

CHAPTER EIGHT

LUCA THREW ASIDE his bow-tie just before he came onto the terrace and bit out, 'Where the hell were you? I've been all over the beachfronts looking for you.'

His anger escalated when he saw Serena put her hands on her hips and say defiantly, 'What was it? Did you think I'd hit some nightclub? Or that I'd gone to find some late-night pharmacy so I could score some meds?'

Luca stopped. He had to acknowledge the relief that was coursing through his veins. She was here. She was safe. But the rawness he felt because she'd walked out on him and looked so upset when he'd suggested she was acting out a charade was still there.

An uncomfortable truth slid into his gut like a knife. Perhaps this *was* her. No charade. No subterfuge.

And just like that, Luca was thrown off-centre all over again.

He breathed deeply. 'I'm sorry.'

Serena was surprised. She blinked. 'Sorry for what?'

Honesty compelled Luca to admit, 'For what I said at the function. I just… *You…*'

He looked away and put his hands on his hips. Suddenly it wasn't so hard to say what he wanted to say—as if something inside him had given way.

He dropped his hands, came closer and shook his head. 'You confound me, Serena DePiero. Everything I thought I knew about you is wrong. The woman who came to Rio, the woman who survived the jungle, the woman who gave those villagers the kind of courtesy not many people ever give them...she's someone I wasn't expecting.'

Serena's ability to think straight was becoming compromised. Emotion was rising at hearing this admission and knowing what it must be costing him.

Huskily she said, 'But this *is* me, Luca. This has always been me. It was just...buried before.' Then she blurted out, 'I'm sorry for running off. I came straight here. I wouldn't have gone near the beaches—not after what you said. I do have *some* street-smarts, you know.'

Luca moved closer. 'I panicked. I thought of you being oblivious to the dangers.'

Now Serena noticed how pale Luca was. *He'd been worried about her.* He hadn't assumed she'd gone off the rails. The anger and hurt drained away, and something shifted inside her. A kind of tenderness welled up. *Dangerous.*

She had to physically resist the urge to go to him and touch his jaw. Instead she said, 'I'm here...safe.'

His hands landed on her hips and he tugged her into him. She was shorter without her heels. He made her feel delicate. Her skin was tingling now, coming up in goosebumps in spite of the warm air. Emboldened by his proximity, and what he'd just said, she lifted her own hands and pushed Luca's jacket apart and down his arms.

He let go of her so that it could fall to the ground.

Without saying anything, Luca took her by the hand and led her into the apartment, stepping over his coat.

Serena let herself be led. She'd never felt this connection with anyone else, and a deep-rooted surge of
desire to reclaim part of her sexuality beat like a drum
in her blood.

Yet when Luca led her into what she assumed was
his bedroom, because of its stark, masculine furnish-
ings, trepidation gripped her. Perhaps she was being
a fool? Reading too much into what he'd said? Didn't
men say *anything* to get women into bed? There was
so much in her past that she was ashamed of, that she
hadn't made peace with, and Luca seemed to have an
unerring ability to bring all of those vulnerabilities to
the fore. What would happen when he possessed her
completely?

Her hand tightened around Luca's and he stopped by
the bed and turned to face her. Serena blurted out the
first thing she could think of, as if to try and put some
space between them again. 'I lost my virginity when I
was sixteen…does that shock you?'

He shrugged, his expression carefully veiled, 'Should
it? I lost mine at sixteen too—when one of my father's
ex-mistresses seduced me.'

Serena's desperation rose, in spite of her shock at
what he'd just revealed so flatly. 'It's what men expect,
though, isn't it? For their lovers to be somehow…in-
nocent?'

Luca made a face. 'I like my lovers to be experienced. I've no desire to be some wide-eyed virgin's
first time.'

A wide-eyed virgin she certainly was *not*. Innocence
had been ripped from her too early.

Luca pulled her closer and heat pulsed into Serena's
lower body. She could feel his arousal between them,

thick and hard. It scattered painful thoughts and she welcomed it like a coward.

'I want you, Serena, more than I've ever wanted anyone. I've wanted you from the first moment I laid eyes on you...'

For a heady moment Serena felt an overwhelming sense of power. She reassured herself that the emotions rising inside her were transitory; sex had never touched her emotionally before, so why should it now?

When he reached for her Serena curled into him without even thinking about it. It felt like the most necessary thing. The world dropped away and it was just them in this tight embrace, hearts thudding, skin hot.

His fingers spread out over her back, making her nipples harden almost painfully against the material of the dress. And then he lowered his head and his mouth was on hers, fitting like the missing piece of a jigsaw puzzle. Serena's lips opened to his on a sigh, tongues touching and tasting, stroking intimately. Her hands wound up around his neck, fingers tugging the short strands of hair, exploring, learning the shape of his skull.

Luca's wicked mouth and tongue made her strain to get even closer. After long, drugging moments he drew back, breathing harshly. Serena had to struggle to open her eyes.

'I want to see you,' he muttered thickly. 'Take down your hair.'

Serena felt as if she was in a dream. Had she, in fact, had this dream more often than once in the past seven years? She lifted her hand to the back of her head, feeling incredibly languid, and removed the discreet pin. Her hair tumbled around her shoulders, making her nerve-ends tingle even more.

Luca reached out and ran his fingers through it, then fisted it in one hand as the other reached around her to draw her into him again, kissing her with ruthless passion, tongue thrusting deep.

Serena's legs were starting to wobble. Luca's mouth was remorseless, sending her brain into a tailspin.

His hands came to the shoulders of her dress and pulled with gentle force, so the material slipped down her arms, loosening around her chest. She broke away from his mouth and looked up into dark pools of blue, feeling insecure.

Her arms came up against her breasts. Luca drew back and gently tugged them away, pulling the front of the dress down, leaving her bared to him.

She wore no bra, and Luca's gaze was so hot her skin sizzled. He reached out a hand and cupped the weight of one breast, a thumb moving over one puckered nipple. She bit her lip to stop from moaning out loud.

And then Luca put his hands on her hips and pulled her into him, hard enough to make her gasp, and replaced his thumb with his mouth, suckling on that hard peak roughly, making her back arch.

His erection was insistent against her and Serena's hips moved of their own volition.

Luca lifted his head. *'Feiticeira.'*

Her tongue felt heavy in her mouth, 'What does that mean?'

'Witch,' Luca replied succinctly.

And he kissed her again before her mind could catch up with the fact that his hands were now pushing her dress down over her hips so that it fell to the floor in a silken swish.

He put one hand between their bodies and Serena

held her breath when he explored down over her belly and lower, until he was gently pushing her legs apart so that he could feel for himself how ready she was.

Serena felt gauche, but wanton, as Luca moved his hand between her legs, over her panties. She lowered her head to his shoulder when her face got hot, and her breathing grew harsher when his wicked fingers moved against her insistently.

He slipped a finger under the gusset of her panties and touched her, flesh to flesh. Serena bit her lip hard enough to make tears spring into her eyes. She wanted to clamp her thighs together—the sensation was too much—but Luca's hand was too strong.

Her legs finally gave way and she collapsed back onto the bed, heart thumping erratically.

Luca started to undo his shirt, revealing that broad and exquisitely muscled chest. A smattering of dark hair covered his pectorals, leading down in a silky line under his trousers to where she could see the bulge of his arousal.

Serena's brain melted and she welcomed it. She didn't want to think or analyse—only feel.

His hands moved to his trousers and he undid them and pushed them down, taking his underwear with them. His erection was awe-inspiring. Long and thick and hard, a bead of moisture at the tip.

'Seven years, Serena,' he said throatily, 'For seven years I've wanted you above any other woman. No one came close to how I imagined this.'

She looked up at him, taken aback. She watched as he reached for something in a drawer in the side table. He rolled protection over his length. There was something unashamedly masculine about the action.

'Lie back,' he instructed gruffly.

Serena did, glad he was giving instructions because she couldn't seem to formulate a single coherent thought.

Luca curled his fingers under the sides of her panties and gently took them off. Now she was naked. And even though she'd been naked in front of men before it had never felt like this. As if she was being reborn.

Luca came down over her on strong arms, their bodies barely touching. He kissed her, and those broad shoulders blocked everything out. Serena reached up, desperate for contact again, her hands touching his chest and moving down the sides of his body, reaching around to his back, sliding over taut, sleek muscles.

Luca broke away. 'You're killing me. I need you… *now*. Spread your legs for me.'

Serena's entire body seemed to spasm at that husky entreaty. She moved her legs apart and Luca came down over her, his body pressing against hers. She could feel the thick blunt head of him pushing against her, seeking entrance.

She opened her legs wider, every cell in her body straining towards this union. Aching for it. She looked up at him, her whole body on the edge of some unknown precipice.

As if some lingering tension shimmering between them had just dissolved, Luca thrust in, hard and deep, and Serena cried out at the exquisite invasion.

It was sore…he was so big…but even as she had that thought the pain was already dissipating to be replaced by a heady sensation of fullness.

'Serena?'

She opened her eyes. Luca was frowning. She hadn't realised that she was biting her lip.

He started to withdraw. 'I've hurt you.'

There was a quality to his voice Serena had never heard before. She gripped him tight with her thighs, trapping him. 'No,' she said huskily. 'You're not hurting me… It's…been a while.'

He stopped, and for an infinitesimal moment Serena thought he was going to withdraw completely. But then he slowly thrust in again and relief rushed through her.

Luca reached under her back, arching her up into him more as he kept up a steady rhythm that made it hard to breathe. She could feel her inner muscles tight around him, saw his gritted jaw, the intense look of concentration on his face.

Luca pressed a searing kiss to her mouth before trailing his lips down, closing them over one nipple and then the other, forcing Serena's back to arch again as spasm after spasm of tiny pleasures rushed through her core.

She locked her feet around the back of Luca's body and he went deeper, but she couldn't break free of that sliver of control that kept her bound, kept her from soaring to the stars. A blinding flash of insight hit her like a smack in the face: she recognised now why she couldn't let go in this moment of intense intimacy— the reason why she'd never let herself feel this deeply before—it was because she'd always been too afraid of losing control.

Which was ironic. But being out of control on drink and medication had been—perversely—*within* her control. This wasn't. This was threatening to wrench her out of herself in a way that was frankly terrifying.

A small sob of need escaped Serena's mouth as that elusive pinnacle seemed to fade into the distance. The turmoil in her chest and body was burning her. But she couldn't let go—even as she heard a guttural sound coming from Luca's mouth and felt his body tense within her before deep tremors shook his big frame and his body thrust against her with the unconscious rhythm of his own release.

She felt hollowed out, unsatisfied.

Luca withdrew from her body, breathing harshly, and Serena winced minutely as her muscles relaxed their tight grip. As soon as Luca released her from the prison of his arms she felt the need to escape and left the bed.

She barely heard him call her name as she shut the bathroom door behind her, locking it. Her legs were shaking and tears burned the back of her eyes as the magnitude of what had just happened sank in. There was something fundamentally flawed, deep inside her. She'd been broken so long ago that she couldn't function normally now. And Luca had to be the one to demonstrate this to her. The ignominy was crushing.

Serena blindly reached into the shower and turned the spray to hot, stepping underneath and lifting her face up to the rush of water. Her tears slid and fell, silent heaves making her body spasm as she let it all out.

She heard banging on the door, her name. She called out hoarsely, 'Leave me alone, Luca!'

And then, mercifully, silence.

Serena sank down onto the floor of the shower as the water beat relentlessly down over her body. She drew her knees up to her chest and dropped her head onto them and tried to tell herself that what had just happened *wasn't* as cataclysmic as she thought it was.

* * *

Luca looked at the locked door. He wasn't used to feeling powerless, but right now he did. He cursed volubly, knowing it wouldn't be heard because he could hear the spray of the shower and something that sounded suspiciously like a sob.

His chest hurt. Was she crying? Had he hurt her?

Luca cursed again and paced. He went to his wardrobe and took out some worn jeans, pulled them on, paced again.

Dammit. No woman had ever reacted like that after making love with him. Running to the bathroom. *Crying.* And yet…

Had he really made love to Serena? Luca asked himself derisively. Or had he been so overcome with lust that he'd not taken any notice of the fact that she clearly hadn't been enjoying herself?

He winced now when he thought of how tight she'd been. And her husky words…*It's…been a while.* To be so tight he'd guess a lot longer than 'a while'. Which meant what? That her reputation for promiscuity was severely flawed, for a start. And she'd been awkward, slightly gauche. Not remotely like the practised seductress he might have expected.

He'd seen how her face had tightened, become inscrutable. She'd shut her eyes, turned her head away… But Luca had been caught in the grip of a pleasure so intense that he'd been unable to hold himself back, releasing himself into her with a force unlike anything he'd known before.

For the first time in his memory Luca was facing the very unpalatable fact that he'd behaved with all the finesse of a rutting bull.

The spray of the shower was turned off and Luca became tense. He felt a very real urge to flee at the prospect of facing Serena now. But that urge stemmed from some deep place he wouldn't acknowledge. She hadn't reached him there. No one had.

When Serena emerged from the bathroom, dressed in a voluminous terrycloth robe, she still felt raw. The bedroom was empty, and a lurch of something awfully like disappointment went through her belly to think that Luca had left.

And then she cursed herself. Hadn't she told him to *'leave me alone'*? Why on earth would he want to have anything to do with a physically and emotionally wounded woman when there had to be any number of willing women who would give him all the satisfaction he might crave without the post-coital angst?

Still…it hurt in a way that it shouldn't.

Serena belted the robe tightly around her waist and, feeling restless, went out to the living area. Her hair lay in a damp tangle down her back.

But when she looked out through the glass doors she saw him. He hadn't left. Her heart stopped as something very warm and treacherous filled her chest.

As she came closer to the open doors she could see that he'd pulled on soft faded jeans. His back was broad and smooth, his hair ruffled. From her hands or the breeze? Serena hovered at the door, on the threshold.

And then Luca said over his shoulder, 'You should come and see the view—it's pretty spectacular.'

Serena came out and stood not far from Luca, putting her hands on the railing. The view was indeed exquisite. Rio was lit up with a thousand lights, the Sugar Loaf in the distance, and the beaches just out of sight. It was magical. Other-worldly.

'I've never seen anything like this,' she breathed, curiously soothed by Luca's muted reaction to her re-appearance.

He said lightly now, 'I find that hard to believe.'

Serena's hands tightened on the railing. 'It's true. Before...I wouldn't have noticed.'

She could sense him turning towards her and her skin warmed. Just like that. From his attention. She glanced at him and his face looked stark in the moon-light.

'Did I hurt you? You were with me all the way and then...you weren't.'

'*No!*' Serena blurted out, horrified that he would think that. 'No,' she said again, quieter, and looked back at the view. 'Nothing like that.'

'Then...what?'

Why wouldn't he let it go? Serena wasn't used to men who gave any consideration to how much she'd enjoyed sex—they'd usually been happy just to say they'd *had* her. The wild child.

Luca's voice broke in again. 'You've already come in my arms, so I know what it feels like, but you shut down.'

Serena got hot, recalling the strength of her orgasm when he'd been touching her in the jungle... But that had been different... He hadn't been *inside her*.

And she hadn't been falling for him.

The realisation hit her now, as if she'd been blocking it out. She *was* falling for him—tumbling, in fact. No

wonder her body had shut down. It had known before
she did. She'd been right to fear his total possession.

She looked at him, shocked, terrified it might be
written over her head in neon lights. But he was just
raising a brow, waiting for an answer. Oblivious.

Her mind whirling with this new and fragile knowledge, she whispered, 'I told you…it's been a while.'

'What's "a while"?'

Serena stared at him, wanting him to let it go.
'Years—okay? A long time.'

Something in his eyes flashed. 'You haven't had any
lovers since you left Italy?'

She shook her head, avoiding his eye again, and said
tightly, 'No—and not for a while before that.'

God, this was excruciating!

'The truth is I've never really enjoyed sex. My reputation for promiscuity and sexual prowess was largely
based on the stories of men who'd been turned down.
I'm afraid I'm not half as debauched as you might
think…a lot of talk and not a lot of action.'

Luca was quiet for a long time, and then he said, 'I
could tell you weren't that experienced. But you were
touted as one of Europe's most licentious socialites and
you didn't do much to defend yourself.'

She sent him a dark glance. 'As if anyone would
have believed me.' She looked out over the view and
felt somehow removed, suspended in space. 'Do you
know how I learned to French kiss?'

She could sense Luca going still. 'How?'

Serena smiled but it was bitter, hard. 'One of my
father's friends. At a party. He came into my room.'

She let out a shocked gasp when Luca grabbed her

shoulders and pulled her around to face him. His face was stark, pale. His reaction took her aback.

'Did he touch you? Did he—?'

Serena shook her head quickly. '*No.* No. My sister Siena was there…we shared a room. She woke up and got into bed beside me and the man left. After that we made sure to lock our door every night.'

Luca's hands were still gripping her shoulders. '*Deus*…Serena.'

He let her go and ran a hand through his hair, looking at her as if she was a stranger. On some deep level Serena welcomed it. The other thing was too scary. Luca looking at her with something approximating gentleness…

She saw a lounger nearby and went over and sat down, pulling her knees up to her chest. Luca stood with his back to the railing, hands in his pockets. Tense.

As if the words were being wrung out of him, he finally said, 'It's not adding up. *You're* not adding up.'

'What's not adding up?' Serena asked quietly, her heart palpitating at Luca's intent look.

'You've had nothing but opportunities to be difficult since you got here and you haven't been. No one can act that well. A child who is medicated for being difficult, wilful…who grows into a wild teenager hell-bent on causing controversy wherever she goes…that's not you.'

Serena's heart beat fast. She felt light-headed. Faintly she said, 'It *was* me.'

Luca was grim. '*Was?* No one changes that easily, or that swiftly.'

He came over and pulled a chair close, sat down. Serena knew her eyes had gone wide. She felt as if she were standing on the edge of a precipice, teetering, about to fall.

'I want to know, Serena… Why were you put on medication so young?'

'I told you…after my mother died—'

Luca shook his head. 'There has to be more to it than that.'

Serena just looked at him. No one had ever been interested in knowing her secrets before. In rehab the professionals had been paid to delve deep, and she'd let them in the interests of getting better.

Luca was pushing her and pushing her—and for what? As if he'd welcome her darkest secrets…

The desire to be vulnerable and allow herself to confide in him in a way she'd never done before made her scared. It was too much, coming on the heels of what had just happened. Realising she was falling in love with him when he was only interested in bedding her. She'd been at pains to let Luca know that this was the real her, and yet she knew well it wasn't. There was a lot more to her. And she couldn't let it out. She felt too fragile.

Acting on a blind instinct to protect herself, Serena stood up abruptly, making Luca tip his head back.

Coldly she said, 'There's nothing more to it—and I thought men didn't like post-coital post-mortems. If we're done here for the evening I'd like to go to bed. I'm tired.'

She went to walk around Luca, her heart hammering, but he grabbed her wrist, stopping her in her tracks. He stood up slowly, eyes narrowed on her.

'What the hell…? *If we're done here for the evening?* What's *that* supposed to mean?'

Serena shrugged and tried to affect as bored a demeanour as possible. 'We've been to the function, we've slept together…' She forced herself to look at him and mocked, 'What more do you want? For me to tuck you in and read you a story?'

Luca's face flushed. He let her wrist go as if it burnt him. He seemed to increase in size in front of her, but instead of intimidating her it only made her more aware of him. He bristled.

'No, sweetheart, I don't want you to tuck me in and read me a story. I want you in my bed at my convenience for as long as I want you.'

He was hard and cruel. And more remote than she could remember ever seeing him. Something inside her curled up tight. But still that instinct to drive him away from seeing too much made her say nonchalantly, 'Well, if it's all the same to you, I'd appreciate spending the rest of the night on my own.'

Liar, her body whispered. Even now between her legs she was getting damp with the desire to feel him surge deep inside her.

So that she could shut down all over again? More humiliation? No, she was doing the right thing.

He came close…close enough to make sweat break out over Serena's skin… If he touched her he'd know how false she was being.

But he stopped just inches away and said, 'We both know that I could have you flat on your back and begging me for release in minutes…a release that you *will* give me next time, Serena.'

He stepped back and Serena felt disorientated. He thought she'd *wilfully* kept herself from being pleasured just to thwart him in some way?

He swept her up and down with a scathing glance. 'But right now I find that my desire has waned.'

He turned and strode back into the apartment and Serena started to shake in reaction. Everything in her wanted to call out to him.

But wasn't this what she wanted? To push him back? The shackles of her past had never felt so burdensome as they did right then. She recognised that they were protecting her, but also imprisoning her.

She could imagine Luca getting changed, walking out through the door, and her gut seized in rejection. Luca was the only person she'd come close to telling everything. She could remember the look on his face just before she'd turned cold. He'd been *concerned*. Until she'd convinced him that she had nothing to say except that she wanted him to leave.

And why wouldn't he leave? He was proud enough to take her at face value. She knew how quickly he damned people—after all he'd damned her for long enough... But that had been changing.

A sense of urgency gripped her—so what if he *did* just want her in his bed? Suddenly Serena knew that in spite of how terrified it made her feel, she desperately wanted to lean on Luca's inherent strength and face these last demons that haunted her still. She was sick of letting her past define her, of being afraid to get too close to anyone in case they saw inside her.

After all, what was the worst that could happen? Luca couldn't look at her any more coldly than he just had. And if he didn't believe her...? Then at least she would have been totally honest.

She heard a movement and saw Luca stride towards the front door, dressed now in black trousers and a black top.

He looked utterly intimidating, but Serena gathered all of her courage, stepped into the apartment again and said, 'Wait, Luca, please. Don't go.'

CHAPTER NINE

LUCA STOPPED AT the door, his hand on the knob. Had he even heard that? Or was it his imagination conjuring up what he wanted to hear from a siren who had him so twisted inside out that he barely knew which way was up any more?

He didn't turn around and forced out a drawl. 'What is it, *minha beleza?* You're ready to come this time?'

He felt dark inside, constricted. He'd really thought he'd seen something incredibly vulnerable in Serena— he'd finally believed that she truly was exactly as she seemed—and then…*wham!* She couldn't have made more of a fool of him if she'd professed undying love and he'd believed her.

There was no sound behind him and he whirled around, anger like a molten surge within him. When he saw the pallor of Serena's cheeks and how huge and bruised her eyes looked he pushed down the concern that rose up to mock him and said scathingly, 'Nice try, *namorada*, but I'm not falling for whatever part you want to play now. Frankly, I prefer a little consistency in my lovers.'

Luca went to turn and leave again, but Serena moved forward jerkily. 'Please, just wait—hear me out.'

He sighed deeply, hating the ball of darkness in his gut. The darkness that whispered to him to run fast and far away from this woman.

He turned around and crossed his arms, arching a brow. 'Well?'

Serena swallowed. Her hair was like a white-gold curtain over her shoulders, touching the swells of her breasts under the robe. Breasts that Luca could taste on his tongue even now.

Incensed that she was catching him like this, and yet still he couldn't walk away, he strode past her over to his drinks cabinet and delivered curtly, 'Spit it out, will you?'

He poured himself a glass of whisky and downed it in one. Hating that she'd even made him feel he needed the sustenance. His hand gripped the glass. He wouldn't look at her again.

'Serena, so help me—'

'You were pushing me to talk…and I didn't want to. So I pretended just now…pretended that I wanted to be alone. I didn't mean what I said, Luca.'

Luca went very still. An inner voice mocked him. *She's still playing you.* But he recalled the way she'd looked so hunted…just before something had come over her expression and she'd morphed into the ice queen in front of his eyes.

Slowly he put the glass down and turned around. Serena looked shaken. Pale. Yet determined.

'I'm sorry.'

Her voice was husky and it touched on his skin like a caress he wanted to rail against.

He folded his arms. 'Sorry for what?'

She bit her lip. 'I wanted you to think that I'd had enough so you'd leave, but that's not true.'

'Tell me something I *don't* know,' Luca drawled, and saw how she went even paler.

He cursed out loud and went over to her, taking her by the arm and leading her to a couch to sit down.

'Serena, so help me God, if this is just some elaborate—'

'It's not!' she cried, her hands gripped together in her lap. 'It's not,' she said again. 'You were just asking me all these things and I felt threatened… I've never told anyone what happened..I've always been too ashamed and guilty that I didn't do something to stop it. And for a long time I doubted that it had even happened…'

Luca knew now that this was no act. Serena was retreating, her mind far away. Instinctively he reached out and took her hands, wrapping them in his. She looked at him and his chest got tight. *Damn her.*

'What happened?'

Her hands were cold in his and her eyes had never looked bigger or bluer.

'I saw my father kill my mother when I was five years old.'

Luca's mouth opened and closed. 'You *what*?'

Serena couldn't seem to take her eyes off Luca, as if he was anchoring her to something. Her throat felt dry.

'When I was five I heard my parents arguing…nothing new…they argued all the time. I sneaked downstairs to the study. When I looked in through the crack of the door I could see my mother crying. I couldn't understand what they were arguing about, although in hindsight I know it was most likely to do with my father's affairs.'

Luca was grim. 'What happened?' he asked again.

'My father backhanded my mother across the face and she fell... She hit her head on the corner of his desk.'

Serena went inward.

'All I can remember is the pool of blood growing around her head on the rug and how dark it was. And how white she was. I must have made a sound, or something. The next thing I remember is my father dragging me back upstairs. I was crying for my mother...hysterical. My father hit me across the face...I remember one of my baby teeth was loose and it fell out... A doctor arrived. He gave me an injection. I can still remember the pain in my arm... The funeral...everything after that... was blurry. Siena was only three. But I can remember the doctor coming a lot. And once the police came. But I couldn't speak to them. I wanted to tell them what I'd seen but I'd been given something that made me sleepy. It didn't seem important any more.'

Her voice turned bitter.

'He got it covered up, of course, and no one ever accused him of her death. That's when it started. By the time I was twelve my father and his doctor were feeding my medication habit. They said I had ADHD—that I was difficult to control. Wilful. That it was for my own good. Then my father started saying things like *bi-polar*. He was constantly perpetuating a myth of mental uncertainty around me—even to my sister, who always believed that I tried to take my own life.'

'Did you?' Luca's voice was sharp.

Serena shook her head. 'No. But even though I denied it my sister was programmed by then to believe in my instability just like everyone else. My father even made a pretence of not allowing me to take drugs for the condition—while he was maintaining a steady supply to me through the doctor on his payroll.'

Luca shook his head. 'But why didn't you leave when you could?'

Serena pushed down the guilt. She had to start forgiving herself.

'I couldn't see a way out. By the time I was sixteen I was living the script my father had written for me years before.'

She reeled off the headlines of the time.

'I was a *wild child. Impossible to tame. Out of control.* And I was addicted to prescription drugs… Siena was innocent. The good girl. Even now Siena still retains an innocence I never had. My father played us off against each other. If Siena stepped out of line I got the punishment…never her. She was being groomed as the perfect heiress. I was being groomed as the car crash happening in slow motion.'

Luca's hands had tightened over hers and it was only then that Serena realised how icy she'd gone.

'Why haven't you ever gone to the police about your mother's death?'

Shame pricked Serena. 'Who would have believed disgraceful, unstable Serena DePiero? It felt hopeless. *I* felt hopeless. And in a way I had begun to doubt myself too…had it really happened? Maybe I was dreaming it up? Maybe I *was* just some vacuous socialite hooked on meds?'

Luca was shaking his head and Serena instantly went colder. She'd been a fool to divulge so much. She pulled her hands back.

'You don't believe me.'

Luca's gaze narrowed and his mouth thinned. 'Oh, I

believe you, all right. It just about makes sense. And I met your father—he was a cold bastard.' He shook his head. 'He turned you into an addict, Serena.'

Something fragile and treacherous unfurled inside Serena. *Acceptance.*

She said huskily, 'I'm sorry about before. I didn't want to tell you everything.'

'So what changed?'

Serena felt as if she was being backed into a corner again, but this time she fought the urge to escape or to push him away. 'You deserved to know the truth, and I was being less than honest.'

'Less than honest about what?'

He was going to make her say it.

Serena was captivated by Luca's gaze. Time seemed to have slowed to a throbbing heartbeat between them. In the same moment she was aware of a giddy rush through her body—a sense of weightlessness. She'd told someone her innermost secrets and the world hadn't crashed around her.

Serena's belly swooped and she took a leap into the void. 'I didn't want to spend the rest of the night alone. It was just an excuse.'

Luca looked at her and something in his eyes darkened. *Desire.* He cupped her face in his hands and slanted his mouth over hers in a kiss so light that it broke Serena apart more than the most passionate kisses they'd exchanged.

When he pulled back she kept him close and whispered shakily, 'Will you stay, Luca?'

She suddenly needed him desperately—needed a way to feel rooted when she might float off altogether and lose touch with the earth.

Luca kissed her mouth again and said throatily, 'Yes.'

He stood and pulled Serena up with him, and then he bent and scooped her into his arms as if she weighed no more than a feather. Her arms moved around his neck but she couldn't resist trailing her fingers along his jaw, and then reaching up to press a kiss against the pulse she could see beating under his bronzed skin.

His chest swelled against her breasts and her whole body pulsed with heat and awareness.

He put her down gently by the rumpled bed, where the scent of their bodies lingered in the air, sultry… Even though they'd already made love Serena was trembling as if they hadn't even touched for the first time.

They came together in a kiss of mutual combustion.

There was no time for Serena to worry about her body letting her down again because she was too feverish for Luca—hands spreading out over his bare chest, nails grazing his nipples, causing him to curse softly. Her hands moved to his trousers, and she unzipped them, freeing his erection. She took him in her hand, relishing the steely strength.

Luca's hands were busy too, opening the belt of the robe and sliding it over her shoulders. Serena looked up at him and took her hands away from his body so that the robe could fall to the floor.

His gaze devoured her…hot. Dark colour slashed his cheeks as he tugged his trousers down and off completely, kicking them aside.

He pushed her gently onto the bed. Serena was shocked at how fast her heart was racing, how ragged her breath was.

Gutturally he said, 'I want to take this slow—not like before.'

But Serena was desperate to feel him again. She was ready. She shook her head and whispered, 'I don't want slow. I want *you*.'

He caught her look and said rawly, 'Are you sure?'

She nodded again, and saw his jaw clench as if he was giving up some thin shred of control. He reached for protection and she watched him smooth it onto his erection, an almost feral look on his face.

Serena's sex pulsed with need. She lifted her arms and beckoned him, spreading her legs in a mute appeal.

His eyes flashed and he muttered something indistinct. He leant down to place his hand on her sex, cupping its heat. Serena found his wide shoulders and gripped him, biting her lip.

He spread his fingers and explored her secret folds, releasing the slick heat of her arousal.

His voice was rough. 'You're so ready for me.'

'Please...' said Serena huskily. 'I want you, Luca.'

Every cell in her body felt engorged with blood as he came down over her, pressing her into the bed, his body hard next to her softness. Crushing it deliciously.

He bent his head and took one pebbled nipple into his mouth, his teeth capturing it for a stinging second before letting go to soothe it with his tongue. This teasing was almost unbearable.

Serena was about to sob out another plea when he pushed his thick length inside her. Her eyes widened and she sucked in a breath as he pushed in, relentless, until he was buried inside her.

'You're so tight...like a vice.' He pressed a kiss to her mouth, hot and musky. 'Relax, *preciosa*...'

The endearment did something to Serena. She felt her body softening around him. He slid even deeper and a look of deep carnal satisfaction crossed his face, making something exult inside her. A sense of her own innately feminine power.

Her nipples scraped against his hair-roughened chest with a delicious friction as Luca started to move in and out, each powerful glide of his body reaching deeper inside Serena to a place she'd locked away long ago. She couldn't take her eyes off him. It was as if he was holding her within his gaze, keeping her rooted in the inexorable building of pleasure.

He reached around to her thigh and brought it up over his hip, his hand smoothing her flesh, then gripping it as his movements became harder, more powerful. That hand crept up and cupped her bottom, kneading, angling her hips, so that he touched some part of her that made her gasp out loud as a tremor of pleasure rocked through her pelvis.

Unconsciously Serena tilted her hips more and Luca moaned deeply. His thrusts became faster and Serena could feel the tight coil of tension inside her, tightening and tightening unbearably, to a point of almost pain.

She was incoherent, only able to stay anchored by looking into Luca's eyes. When she closed hers briefly he commanded roughly, 'Look at me, Serena.'

She did. And something broke apart deep inside her.

Her whole body tautened against his, nerves stretched to screaming point. Luca moved his hand between them, his fingers finding the engorged centre of her desire, and he touched her with a precision that left her nowhere to hide or hang on to. She imploded. Her control was shattered—the control she'd clung to all her life. Since her world had fallen apart as a child, when being *out* of control had become her control.

In one instant it was decimated, and Serena soared high on a wave of bliss that was spectacular. The definition of an orgasm being a *petit mort*, a small death, had never felt so apt. She knew that a part of her had just died and something else incredibly fragile and nebulous was taking its place.

She floated back down to reality, aware of her body milking Luca's own release as he shuddered and buried his head in her shoulder, his body embedded deep within hers. Her legs wrapped around him, and the pulsations of their mutual climaxes took long minutes to die away.

Luca was in the kitchen the following morning, making breakfast, before he realised that he'd never in his life made breakfast for a lover. In general he liked being in a situation where he could extricate himself rather than have to deal with the aftermath and unwelcome romantic projections.

But here he was, cooking breakfast for Serena without half a second's hesitation or any desire to put as much space between them as possible. His head was still fuzzy from an overload of sensual pleasure and the revelations she'd made.

He couldn't help thinking of her: a little girl, traumatised by the violent death of her mother, with a sadistic and mercurial father who tried to discredit her as soon as he could. Somehow it wasn't that fantastical to believe her father capable of such things.

He thought back to that night when he'd watched Siena come to bail Serena out of jail. The way she had tended to Serena like a mother to her cub…the way Serena had leant on her as if it was a familiar pattern.

Both had been manipulated by their father's machinations. Both had been acting out their parts. The good
girl and the bad girl.

It all made a sick kind of sense now, because Luca
knew he hadn't imagined the vulnerability he'd sensed
about her that night he'd first met her...

A sound from behind him made him tense and he
turned around to see Serena, tousle-haired and dressed
in the robe, standing in the doorway. She looked hesitant, shy, and Luca was falling, losing his grip. Everything he thought he'd known about her...*wasn't*.

His hands gripped the bowl he was using to whisk
eggs. 'Hungry?'

'Starving.'

Serena's voice was husky, and it fired up Luca's
blood, reminding him of how she'd shouted out his
name in the throes of passion just short hours before.
How she'd begged and pleaded with him. How she'd
felt around him.

Deus.

Serena came into the kitchen feeling ridiculously shy.
Luca looked stern, intense.

'I didn't know you cooked.'

Luca grimaced in a half-smile, some of the intensity
in his expression diminishing slightly as he continued
whisking. 'I don't...I have a very limited repertoire and
scrambled eggs is about as haute cuisine as it gets.'

Serena sat up on a stool by the island and tried not
to let herself melt too much at seeing Luca in such a
domestic setting in worn jeans and a T-shirt, his hair
mussed up and a dark growth of stubble on his jaw.

'Where did you learn?'

He was taking thin strips of bacon now, and placing them under a hot grill. He didn't look at her. 'When my mother left, my father let the housekeeper go; he always felt it was an unnecessary expense.'

Serena felt indignation rise. 'But how did you cope? Did your father cook?'

Luca shook his head. 'I was at boarding school outside Rio for most of the time, so it was only the holidays when I had to fend for myself.' His mouth twisted. 'One of my father's many mistresses took pity on me when she found me eating dry cereal. She taught me some basics. I liked her—she was one of the nicer ones—but she left.'

More sharply than she'd intended, Serena said, 'She wasn't the one who seduced you?'

Luca looked at her, a small smile playing around his hard mouth. 'No.'

Embarrassed by the surge of jealousy, Serena said, 'Your father never married again?'

'No.'

Luca poured some delicious-smelling coffee out of a pot into big mugs, handing her one. Serena bent her head to smell deeply.

'He learnt his lesson after my mother walked away with a small fortune. She'd come from money in Italy, but by then it was almost all gone.'

Serena thought of his parents not even caring which boy went with who and felt sad. She remarked almost to herself, 'I can't imagine how I would have coped if Siena and I had been separated.'

Luca put a plate full of fluffy scrambled eggs and crispy bacon in front of Serena. He looked at her as he settled on his own stool. 'You're close, aren't you?'

Serena nodded, emotional for a second at the thought of her sister and her family. 'Yes, she saved me.'

Luca's gaze sharpened. 'It sounds to me like you saved yourself, as soon as you could.'

Serena shrugged minutely, embarrassed again under Luca's regard. 'I guess I did.' She swallowed some of the delicious food and asked curiously, 'Is your twin brother like you? Determined to right the wrongs of the world?'

Luca sighed heavily. 'Max is…complicated. He resented me for a long time because my father insisted on leaving everything to me—even though I tried to give him half when our father died. He was too proud to take it.'

Serena shook her head in disbelief, and was more than touched to know that Luca had been generous enough to do that.

'He had a tougher time than me—our mother was completely unstable, lurching from rich man to rich man in a bid to feather her nest, and in and out of rehab. Max went from being enrolled in an exclusive Swiss boarding school to living on the streets in Rome…'

Serena's eyes widened.

'He pulled himself out of the gutter with little or no help; he wouldn't accept any from me and he certainly wouldn't take it from my father. It was only years later, when he'd made his first million, that we could meet on common ground.'

Serena put down her knife and fork. Luca had shown signs of such intransigence and an inability to forgive when she'd first come to Rio, but now she was seeing far deeper into the man and realising he'd had just as much of a complicated background as she had in many respects. And yet he'd emerged without being tainted by the corruption of his father, or by the vagaries of his mother—vagaries that she understood far too well.

For the first time Serena had to concede that perhaps she hadn't done too badly, considering how easy it would have been to insist on living in a fog, not dealing with reality.

Luca was looking at her with an eyebrow raised. He was waiting for an answer to a question she hadn't heard. She blushed. 'Sorry. I was a million miles away.'

'You said when you first got here that you wanted to see Rio?'

Serena nodded, not sure where this was going or what might happen after last night.

'Well…'

Luca was exhibiting a tiny glimmer of a lack of his usual arrogance and it set Serena's heart beating fast.

'It's the weekend. I'd like to show you Rio.'

The bottom seemed to drop out of Serena's stomach. She felt ridiculously shy again. Something bubbled up inside her—lightness. *Happiness*. It was alien enough to take her by surprise.

'Okay, I'd like that.'

CHAPTER TEN

'HAD ENOUGH YET?'

Serena mumbled something indistinct. This was paradise. Lying on Ipanema Beach as the fading rays of the sun baked her skin and body in delicious heat. There was a low hum of conversation from nearby, the beautiful sing-song cadence of Portuguese, people were laughing, sighing, talking. The surf of the sea was crashing against the shore.

And then she felt Luca's mouth on hers and her whole body orientated itself towards his. She opened her eyes with an effort to find him looking down at her. Her heart flip-flopped. She smiled.

'Can we stay for the sunset?'

Luca was trying to hang on to some semblance of normality when the day that had just passed had veered out of *normal* for him on so many levels it was scary.

'Sure,' he said, with an easiness belying his trepidation. Serena's open smile was doing little to restore any sense of equilibrium.

One day spent walking around Rio and then a couple of hours on the beach was all it had taken to touch her skin with a luminous golden glow. Her hair looked blonder, almost white, her blue eyes were standing out even more starkly.

That morning they had taken the train up through the forest to the Cristo Redentor on Corcovado and Serena had been captivated by every tiny thing. Standing at the railing, looking down over the breathtaking panorama of Rio, she'd turned to him and asked, with a look of gleaming excitement that had reminded him of a child, 'Can we go to the beach later?'

Luca's insides had tightened ominously. She didn't want to go shopping. She wanted to see Rio. Genuinely.

Before they'd hit the beach they'd eaten lunch at a favourite café of Luca's. At one point he'd sat back and asked, with an increasing sense of defeat, 'Your family really aren't funding you...are they?'

Immediate affront had lit up those piercing eyes. Luca wouldn't have believed it before. But he did now, and it had made something feel dark and heavy inside him.

'Of course not.' She'd flushed then, guiltily, and admitted with clear reluctance, 'My sister and her husband paid for an apartment for me in Athens...when I was ready to move on. But I'm going to pay them back as soon as I've made enough money.'

Darkness had twisted inside Luca. People got handouts all the time from family, yet she clearly hated to admit it. And this was a woman who had had everything...a vast fortune to inherit...only to lose it all.

She'd flushed self-consciously when she'd caught him looking at her cleared plate of *feijoãda*, a famous Brazilian stew made with black beans and pork. 'My sister is the same. It's a reaction to the tiny portions of food we were allowed to eat by our father, growing up.'

Her revelation had hit him hard again. The sheer abuse her father had subjected her to. Anger still simmered in his belly. Luca had felt compelled to reach out and take her hand, entwining his fingers with hers—something that had felt far too easy and necessary.

'Believe me, it's refreshing to see a woman enjoy her food.'

Her hand had tensed in his and she'd said, far too lightly, while avoiding his eyes, 'I'm sure the women you know are far more restrained.'

Was she jealous? The suspicion had caught at Luca somewhere deeply masculine. And that deeply masculine part of him had been triggered again when he'd insisted on buying her a bikini so she could swim at the beach, as they hadn't been prepared.

He took her in now, as she lay beside him, the three tiny black triangles doing little to help keep his libido in check. He was just glad that the board shorts he'd bought to swim in were roomy enough to disguise his rampant response.

As if aware of his scrutiny Serena fidgeted, trying to pull the bikini over her breasts more—which only made some of the voluptuous flesh swell out at the other side.

Luca bit back a groan.

She'd hissed at him in the shop, 'I'm not wearing that—it's indecent!'

Luca had drawled wryly, 'Believe me, when you see what most women wear on the beaches here you'll feel overdressed.'

And when they'd hit the sand Serena's reaction had been priceless. Mouth open, eyes popping out of her head, she'd watched the undeniably sensual parade of beautiful bodies up and down the beach.

Luca hadn't been unaware of the blatant interest her pale blonde beauty had attracted, and had stared down numerous men.

The sun was setting now, and people were starting to cheer and clap as it spread out in a red ball of fire over the horizon, just to the left of one of Rio's craggy peaks.

Serena sat up and drew her legs to her chest, wrapping her arms around them. She smiled at Luca, before taking in the stunning sunset and clapping herself. 'I love how they do that.'

Her pleasure in something so simple mocked his deeply rooted cynicism. And then Luca realised then that he was enjoying this too, but it had been a long time since he'd taken the time to appreciate it. Even when he'd been younger he'd been so driven to try and counteract his father's corrupt legacy that he'd rarely taken any time out for himself. He'd fallen into a pattern of choosing willing women who were happy with no-strings-attached sex to alleviate any frustration.

He'd never relaxed like this in a typical *carioca* way, with a beautiful woman.

The sun had set and she looked at him now, and all he could see was the damp golden hair trailing over her shoulders, close to the full thrust of her breasts. Her mouth, like a crushed rose petal, was begging to be tasted. And those wide eyes were looking at him with a wariness that only fired his libido even more.

He said roughly, 'Let's get out of here.'

Serena couldn't mistake the carnal intent in Luca's eyes. He'd been looking at her all day as if he'd never seen her before. And today…today had been like a dream.

Her skin felt tight from the sun and sea, and she

didn't know if it was just Luca's unique effect on her, or the result of watching the Rio natives embrace their sensuality and sexuality all afternoon, but right now she trembled with the sexual need that pulsed through her very core and blood.

'Yes,' she said.

She stood up, and Luca stood too, handing her the sundress she'd put on that morning.

They walked the short distance back to Luca's car and when he took her hand in his, Serena's fingers tightened around his reflexively. He wore an open shirt over his chest, still in his shorts, and her heart clenched because he looked so much younger and more carefree than the stern, intimidating man she'd met again the day she'd arrived in Rio.

When they began winding up through the hills, away from the beaches, Serena asked, 'Where is this?'

Luca glanced at her. 'We're going to my home in Alto Gavea. It's closer.'

Serena's heart beat fast. *His home.*

The rest of the drive was in silence, as if words were superfluous and might not even penetrate the thick sensual tension between them.

This part of Rio was encased in forest, reminding Serena of the rainforest with a sharp poignancy. And Luca's home took her breath away when he turned in to a long secluded drive behind fortified gates.

It was an old colonial house, two-storey, white, with terracotta slates on the roof, and it was set, literally, in the middle of the lush Tijuca Forest.

He pulled the car to a stop and looked at her for a long moment. They were suspended in time, with no sounds except for the calls of some birds.

Then he broke the spell and got out of the car, helping Serena out of the low-slung seat. She let out a small
squeal of surprise when he scooped her up into his arms
and navigated opening the front door with commend-
able dexterity.

He took the stairs two at a time and strode into a
massive bedroom. Serena only had time to take in an
impression of a house that was cool and understated.
In his room, the open shutters framed a view showcasing the illuminated Christ the Redeemer statue in the
far distance on its hill overlooking Rio.

Everything became a little dream-like after that,
and Serena knew that on some level she was shying
away from analysing the significance of the day that
had passed.

Luca put her down, only to disappear into a bathroom, where she heard the sound of a shower running.
When he emerged he was taking off his clothes until
he stood before her naked, unashamedly masculine and
proud.

'Come here.'

She obeyed without question. When she stood before him he reached down for the hem of her dress and
pulled it up and off. Then he turned her around and
undid her flimsy bikini top so that it fell to the floor.

He turned her back and hooked his fingers into the
bottoms, and pulled them down until she could step
out of them at her feet. In that moment, naked, she'd
never felt more womanly or more whole. Or more free
of the shadows that had dogged her for as long as she
could remember. They weren't gone completely, but it
was enough for now.

He took her hand and led her into the bathroom,

which was fogged with steam that curled over their sticky, sandy bodies. Standing under the hot spray, Serena lifted her face and Luca covered her mouth with his, his huge body making the space tiny.

When he took his mouth off hers she opened her eyes to see his hot gaze devouring her. And just like that she was ready, her body ripening and moistening for him, ravenous at the sight of Luca's gleaming wet and aroused body. He lifted her and instructed her to put her legs around him—then groaned and stopped.

She looked at him, breathless with anticipation. 'What's wrong?'

'No protection, *preciosa*. We need to move.'

Serena was dazed as he carried her out of the shower, her legs still wrapped around his waist. She could see the pain on his face at the interruption but she was glad… She'd been too far gone to think about protection herself.

He put her down on the bed and reached for a condom from his cabinet, ripping the foil and sheathing himself with big, capable hands. Serena felt completely wanton as she watched this display of masculine virility.

And then he was coming back down over her, pushing her legs apart, settling between them, asking huskily, 'Okay?'

She nodded, her chest tightening ominously, and then Luca was thrusting in so deep her back arched and her legs went around his waist. It was fast and furious, his gaze holding hers, not letting her look away.

Bliss broke over her after mere minutes. She was so primed—as if now it was the easiest thing in the world and not something that had been torturously elusive when they'd first made love.

Serena bit into Luca's shoulder as powerful spasms racked her body just as he reached his own climax, his body thrusting rhythmically against hers until he was spent. He collapsed over her and she tightened her arms and legs around him, loving the feel of him pressing her into the bed, his body still big inside hers.

Eventually he withdrew, and Serena winced as her muscles protested. Luca collapsed on his back beside her, his breathing as uneven as hers. She looked at him to find him watching her with a small enigmatic smile playing around his mouth.

He came up on one arm and touched his fingers to her jaw. 'You make me lose my mind every time...' he admitted gruffly.

Serena looked at him. Somehow his confession wasn't as comforting as she'd thought it might be. It left her with a definite sense that Luca did not welcome such a revelation.

And then he was kissing her again, wiping everything from her mind, and she welcomed it weakly. She was far too afraid to face the suspicion that she had fallen in love with this man and there was no going back.

Three days later

'Miss DePiero? Senhor Fonseca said to let you know that he's been unavoidably detained and you should eat without him.'

'Okay, thank you.' Serena put down the kitchen phone extension and looked at the chicken stew she'd made, bubbling on the state-of-the-art cooker. *Unavoidably detained.* What was that code for?

Crazy to feel so disappointed, but she did. She'd spent her lunch hour buying ingredients, and as soon as she'd finished work at the charity office she'd rushed back to start cooking.

And now she felt ridiculous—because wasn't this such a cliché? The little woman at home, cooking dinner for her man and getting all bent out of shape because it was spoiled?

Mortified at the thought of what Luca's reaction would have been to see this attempt at creating some kind of domestic idyll, and losing any appetite herself, Serena took the chicken stew off the cooker. When it had cooled sufficiently she resisted the urge to throw it away and put it into a bowl to store in the fridge.

Feeling antsy, she headed outside to the terrace. The stunning view soothed her in a way that Athens had never done, even though she now called it home.

'Maledire,' she cursed softly in Italian. And then she cursed Luca, for making her fall for him.

The weekend had been...*amazing.* She remembered Luca kissing the tattoo on her shoulder. He'd murmured to her, 'You know the swallow represents resurrection?'

Serena had nodded her head, feeling absurdly emotional that he *got it.*

When they'd woken late on Sunday Luca had told her that he had to visit a local *favela* and she'd asked to go with him. She had seen first-hand his commitment to his own city. The amazing Fonseca Community Centre that provided literacy classes, language classes, business classes and a crèche so that everyone in the community could learn.

When she'd gone wandering, left alone briefly, she'd found Luca in the middle of a ring of men, doing *capoeira*, a Brazilian form of martial arts. He'd been stripped to the waist, his torso gleaming with exertion, making graceful and unbelievably agile movements to the beat of a drum played by a young boy.

She hadn't been the only woman ogling his spectacular form. By the time he'd finished, a gaggle of women and girls had been giggling and blushing. But a trickle of foreboding had skated over her skin... That had been the moment when he'd caught her eye and she'd seen something indecipherable cross his face. By the time he'd caught up with her again there had been something different about him. He'd shut down.

He'd brought her back here, to this apartment, and even though he'd stayed the night and made love to her, something had been off. When she'd woken he'd been gone, and she hadn't seen him again until late that evening, when he'd arrived and, with an almost feral look on his face, had kissed her so passionately that all tendrils of concern had fled, to be replaced with heat, distracting her from the fact that he clearly hadn't been interested in anything else.

The truth was that every moment she spent with Luca was ripping her apart internally. Especially when he looked at her as if she were some kind of unexploded device, yet kissed her as if his life depended on it. Clearly he was conflicted about her. He'd admitted that it was hard for him to come to terms with the fact that she wasn't what he'd believed her to be. And Serena had the gut-wrenching feeling that Luca would have almost preferred it if she *had* been the debauched, spoilt princess he'd expected.

She had to face the fact that her confession, while

liberating for her, had not proved to be so cataclysmic for Luca.

And of *course* it wouldn't have been, Serena chided herself. For Luca this was just…an affair. A slaking of desire. The fact that it had brought about her own personal epiphany was all Serena would have to comfort her when it was over, and that would have to be enough.

When Luca walked into the apartment it was after midnight. He felt guilty. He knew Serena had been making dinner because she'd told him earlier, when he'd seen her on a visit to the charity offices. It was a visit that had had his employees looking at him in surprise, because he usually conducted meetings in his own office and had little cause to visit them.

The apartment was silent, but he could smell the faint scent of something delicious in the air. When he went into the kitchen it was pristine, but he opened the fridge and saw the earthenware bowl containing dinner. The thought that perhaps she hadn't eaten because he hadn't been there made him feel guiltier. He hadn't even known that Serena could cook until she'd told him she'd taken lessons in Athens.

And he hadn't known how deeply enmeshed he was becoming with her until he'd looked at her in the *favela* and the enormity of it all had hit him. It had taken seeing her against that dusty backdrop—Serena DePiero, ex-socialite and wild child, looking as comfortable in the incongruous surroundings as if she'd been born into them like a native. In spite of the white-blonde beauty that had set her apart. He'd certainly been aware of the men looking at her, and the same black emotion that had gripped him at the beach had caught him again.

Jealousy. For the first time.

It was in that moment that a very belated sense of exposure had come over him and made him pull back from a dangerous brink. Luca knew better than anyone how fickle people were—how you couldn't trust that they wouldn't just pull your world out from under your feet within seconds.

His own parents had done it to him and his brother—setting them on different paths of fate almost as idly as if they were Greek gods, playing with hapless mortals. For years he'd had nightmares about his parents pulling them limb from limb, until their body parts were so mixed up that they didn't even know who was who any more.

Serena was getting too close—under his skin. Everything kept coming back to how badly he'd misjudged her—and never more so than now. He'd just had a conversation with his brother, who was in Rio on business.

And yet as he stood in the doorway of her bedroom now and saw the shape of her under the covers, the bright splash of white-blonde hair, he was taking off his clothes before he even realised what he was doing, sliding in behind her, wrapping himself around her and trying desperately to ignore the way his soul felt inexplicably soothed.

Even as she woke and turned towards him, her seeking sleepy mouth finding his, Luca was steeling himself inside—because this would all be over as soon as she knew what his brother had just told him. Because then everything that had bound them from the past would be gone.

But just…not yet.

When Serena woke in the dawn light, the bed was empty. But the hum in her body and the pleasurable ache between her legs told her she hadn't dreamt that Luca had come into her bed last night. Or dreamt the mindless passion he'd driven her to, taking her over the edge again and again, until she'd been spent, exhausted, begging for mercy.

It was as if Luca had been driven by something desperate.

She blinked, slowly coming awake. And even though her body was sated and lethargic from passion, her heart was heavy. She loved Luca, and she knew with cold certainty that he didn't love her. But he wanted her.

His love was his commitment to the environment, to making the world a better place in whatever small way he could, born from his zeal not to be like his predecessors—a zeal she could empathise with.

And Serena knew that she wouldn't be able to continue falling deeper and deeper without recognising that the heartbreak would be so much worse when she walked away.

It was only when she sighed deeply and moved her head that she felt something, and looked to see a note on the pillow beside her.

She reached for the thick paper and opened it to read:

Please meet me in my office when you wake. L.

A definite shiver of foreboding tightened Serena's skin. No wonder there had been something desperate in Luca's lovemaking last night. This was it. He was going to tell her it was over. The signs had been there for the last few days, since the *favela*.

Anger lanced her. To think that he would just send her away so summarily after sating his desire, which was obviously on the wane, and after she'd enjoyed working in the charity office so much. But, as much as she'd come to love Rio de Janeiro, she didn't relish the thought of being in such close proximity to him in the future—seeing him get on with his life, take another lover.

She wasn't going to let him discard her completely, though; no matter what had happened between them personally he owed her a job. In any event, she knew now that she had to go home. So, while Luca might be preparing to let her go, Serena told herself stoutly that she was ready.

It was only when she noticed her hands trembling in the shower that she had to admit her anger was stemming from a place of deep fear that she was about to feel pain such as she'd never felt before—not even when she'd been at her lowest ebb, trapped by her addictions. Before, she'd anaesthetised herself against the pain. Now she would have nothing to cling on to, and she wasn't sure how ready she was to cope with that.

CHAPTER ELEVEN

WHEN SERENA KNOCKED on Luca's office door about an hour later she felt composed, dressed in plain trousers and a silk shirt. Hair tied back. It had been a mere two weeks since she'd come here for the first time, but she was a different person.

Damn him.

His assistant opened the door and ushered her in, and it took a second after the girl had left for Serena to realise that there was another man in the room. He was standing on the other side of Luca's desk, and Luca stood up now from his high-backed chair.

'Serena—come in.'

Her heart lurched. So formal. For a crazy moment Serena wondered if the other man was a solicitor, so that Luca could get out of the contract?

When she came closer, though, she saw a resemblance between the two men, even though this man had tawny eyes and dark blond messy hair. They were almost identical in size and build. The stranger was as arrestingly gorgeous as Luca, but in a more traditional way—in spite of the scar she could see running from his temple to his jaw. He oozed danger, even though he looked as if he might have stepped from the pages of Italian *Vogue* in an immaculate dark suit.

She sensed a subtle tension in the air, and had just realised herself who he was when Luca said, 'This is my brother—Max Fonseca Roselli.'

She came forward and took the hand offered to her, suffering none of the physical reaction Luca caused within her with only a look. Even so, she saw the unmistakably appreciative gleam in his unusual golden-green eyes and could well imagine that he must leave a trail of bleeding hearts wherever he went. He had that same indomitable arrogance that Luca wore so well.

'Nice to meet you.'

His hand squeezed hers. 'You too.'

Serena pulled away, getting hot, sensing Luca's intense focus on them and Max's desire to needle his brother. When she looked at Luca, though, he gave nothing away and she cursed herself. Of *course* he wouldn't be proprietorial or jealous.

Luca indicated for them to sit down and said heavily, 'Max has some news for you...and me. I thought I owed it to you to let him tell you face to face.'

Now Serena was nervous, and she looked from him to Max and back. 'What is it?'

Luca explained. 'I asked Max to look into what happened at the club that night—to do some digging.'

Before she could properly assimilate that information, Max drawled in a deep voice, 'My brother knows I have some...less than legitimate connections.'

Serena looked at him and her heart went out to both of them for what they'd been through as children. The way their parents had all but rolled the dice to decide their fate.

Huskily she admitted, 'I... Luca told me what happened.'

Max's eyes flared and he shot his brother a scowl.

Luca said warningly, 'This isn't about *us*.'

For a second Serena could have laughed. They might not be identical, but right then she could see how similar they were—and they probably didn't even know it themselves.

Max looked back to her. 'I did some digging and discovered who did plant the drugs on Luca that night. He was a small-time dealer and in the crush he spotted you together. He knew that if he could plant the drugs on you or Luca no one would ever dispute that you had been involved.'

Shame lanced Serena to be reminded that everyone knew of her exploits and how tarnished her reputation was, even as her heart beat fast and she wondered why Luca had asked his brother to do this.

Max continued. 'He's actually in jail at the moment on another charge, and he's been bragging to anyone who will listen about how he set you and Luca up— it would appear that he couldn't bear to keep such a coup to himself. He's been charged with the offence and hasn't a leg to stand on because he's confessed to so many witnesses.'

For a moment the relief was so enormous that Serena felt dizzy, even though she was sitting down. She looked at Luca, whose face was stern. 'You can clear your name.'

He nodded, but he didn't look happy about it. He looked grim.

Max stood up, rising with athletic grace. 'My flight leaves in a couple of hours. I have to go.'

Serena stood up too. 'Thank you so much. This means…a lot.'

Max inclined his head before sending an enigmatic look to his brother. 'I'll be in touch.'

Luca nodded. They didn't embrace or shake hands before Max left, striding out with that same confident grace as his brother.

When he was gone, Serena sank down onto the chair, her head in a spin. She looked at Luca, barely taking in that he looked a little pale, his face all lean lines. 'How...? Why did you ask him to do this?'

He sighed heavily. 'Because I owed it to you to find out the truth. After all, you've been nothing but honest with me. The fact is that I think I suspected you were innocent in the jungle. This just proves that you were as much a victim as I was. You deserve to have your life back, Serena. And you deserve to have the slate cleared too. My lawyers and my PR team will make sure this is in all the papers.'

Serena felt an almost overwhelming surge of emotion to think that Luca was going out of his way to clear her name too. Perhaps now people wouldn't always associate her with feckless debauchery.

Treacherously, this made her hope for too much, even when *The End* was written into every tense line of Luca's body. Clearly he just wanted to move on now.

It made her want to push him away again, for making her feel too much. For making her fall in love. *Damn him.*

'And if Max hadn't found the culprit so easily? Would you have believed me anyway?'

Luca stood up and paced behind his desk, his white shirt pulled across his chest, trousers hugging slim hips. Just like that, heat flared in Serena's solar plexus.

He stopped and looked at her. 'Yes.'

Serena cursed herself for pushing him. She hated

herself for the doubt, for thinking that he was lying. And then she had to concede that Luca *didn't* lie. He was too moral. Too damn good.

She stood up again, her legs wobbly. 'Well, thank you for finding out.'

Luca looked at her for a long moment, and then he said, 'Serena—'

She put up her hand, because she couldn't bear for him to say it. 'Wait. I have something I need to tell you first.'

His mouth closed and he folded his arms across his chest. Serena knew she couldn't be anything else other than completely honest. She had been through too much soul-searching to ever want to hide away from pain again. She might never see him again. The urge to tell him how she felt was rising like an unstoppable wave.

'I've fallen in love with you, Luca.'

He looked at her, and as she watched, the colour leached from his face. She broke apart inside, but was determined not to show it.

'I know it's the last thing you want to hear. We were only ever about...' she stalled '...not *that*...and I know it's over.'

She gestured with a hand to where Max had been sitting.

'After this...we owe each other nothing. And I'm sorry again that your association with me made things bad for you.'

Luca unfolded his arms and slashed a hand in the air, looking angry. 'You don't have to apologise—if I hadn't been so caught up in blaming you, I would have ensured a proper investigation was carried out years ago. You had to suffer the stigma of those accusations too.'

Serena smiled bitterly. 'I was used to it, though. I had no reputation to defend.'

'No—your father took care of that.'

Responsibility weighed heavily on her shoulders. 'I have to go home… I have to tell people about my father—see that he's brought to justice finally.'

'If there's anything you need help with, please let me know.'

Her heart twisted. So polite. So courteous. A million miles from their first meeting in this office. And even though she knew her own family would be there to back her up, she felt an awful quiver of vulnerability—because, really, the only person she wanted by her side the day she faced her father again was Luca.

But that scenario was not to be part of her future.

She hitched up her chin and tried to block out the fact that she'd told Luca she loved him and had received no similar declaration in return. That fantasy belonged deep where she harboured dreams of the kind of fulfilment and happiness she saw her sister experiencing with her family. But at least she could take one good thing with her.

'Are you still going to give me a job?'

'Of course—wherever you want,' Luca said quickly, making another piece of Serena's heart shatter. He was obviously *that* eager to see her go.

'I'd like to go back to Athens today.'

Luca said tightly, 'Laura will arrange it for you.'

'Thank you.'

So clipped, so polite.

Before anger could rise at Luca's non-reaction to her baring her soul to him, she turned to leave.

She was at the door before she heard a broken-sounding, 'Serena...'

Heart thumping, hope spiralling, Serena turned around. Luca looked tortured.

But he said only two words. 'I'm sorry.'

Her heart sank like a stone. She knew he didn't love her, but she marvelled that the human spirit was such an irrepressibly optimistic thing even in the face of certain disappointment.

She forced a smile. 'Don't be. You've given me the gift of discovering how strong I am.'

You've given me the gift of discovering how strong I am.

Luca was stuck in a state of paralysis for so long after Serena left that he had to blink and focus to realise that Laura was in his office and speaking to him, looking worried.

'Senhor Fonseca? Are you all right?'

And as if he'd been holding something at bay, it ripped through him then, stunning and painful in its intensity, like warmth seeping into frozen limbs. Burning.

'No,' he issued curtly, going over to his drinks cabinet and helping himself to a shot of whisky.

When he turned around, Laura's eyes were huge and she was pale. And Luca knew he was coming apart at the seams.

He forced himself not to snarl at the girl, but the pain inside him was almost crippling. 'What is it?'

Laura stuttered, making him feel even worse. 'It's—it's Miss DePiero. I just thought you'd want to know she's on her way to the airport. She's booked first class on a flight to Athens this afternoon.'

'Thank you,' Luca bit out. 'I'm going to be unavailable for the rest of the day. Please cancel all my appointments. Go home early if you want.'

Laura blinked and said faintly, 'Yes, sir.' And then backed away as if he might explode.

He waited until Laura had left and then left himself, knowing nothing more than that he needed to get out—get away. Because he felt like a wounded animal that might lash out and cause serious harm.

He was aware of one or two people approaching him as he walked out of the building, but they quickly diverted when they saw his face. He walked and walked without even knowing where he was going until he realised he was at Ipanema Beach. Where he'd taken Serena just a few days ago.

The scene was the same, even during the week. The beautiful bodies. The amorous couples. The crashing waves. But it mocked him now, for feeling so carefree that day. For believing for a moment that he could be like those people. That he could *feel* like them.

Anger rose up as he ripped off his tie and jacket, dropping them on a bench and sitting down. That was the problem. He knew he couldn't feel. The ability had been cut out of him the day he and his brother had been torn apart.

As young boys they'd been close enough to have a special language that only they understood. It had used to drive their father crazy. And Luca could remember that they'd sensed something was happening that day when their parents had brought them into their father's study.

Luca's mother had bent down to his level and said, with the scent of alcohol on her breath, 'Luca, darling,

I love you so much I want to take you to Italy with me. Will you come?'

He'd looked at Max, standing near his father. Luca had known that Max loved their mother—he had too—but he didn't like it when she came home drunk and falling down. He and Max would fight about it—Max hating it if Luca said anything critical, which he was more liable to do.

He'd looked back at his mother, confused. 'But what about Max? Don't you love him too?'

She'd been impatient. 'Of course I do. But Max will stay here with your father.'

Panic had clutched at his insides, making him feel for a moment as if his bowels might drop out of his body. 'For ever?'

She'd nodded and said, slurring slightly, 'Yes, *caro,* for ever. We don't need them, do we?'

Luca had heard a noise and looked to see Max, ashen, eyes glimmering with tears. 'Mamma...?'

She'd made an irritated sound and said something in rapid Italian, taking Luca by the hand forcibly, as if to drag him out. Luca had felt as if he was in some kind of nightmare. Max had started crying in earnest and had run to their mother, clutching at her waist. That was when Luca had felt some kind of icy calm come over him—as if Max was acting out how he felt deep inside, but he couldn't let it out. It was too huge.

His mother had issued another stream of Italian and let Luca go, shoving him towards his father, prising Max off her and saying angrily, '*Bastante!* Stop snivelling. I'll take you with me instead. After all,' she'd said snidely over Max's hiccups, 'your father doesn't care *who* he gets...'

The black memory faded. His mother had told him she loved him and then minutes later she'd demonstrated how empty her words were. Swapping one brother for the other as if choosing objects in a shop.

Serena had told him she loved him.

As soon as she'd said the words, Luca had been transported back to that room, closing in on himself, waiting for the moment when she'd turn around and show him that she didn't mean it. Not really. She was only saying it because that was what women did, wasn't it? They had no idea of the devastation they could cause when the emptiness of their words was revealed.

But she hadn't looked blasé. Nor as if she hadn't meant it. She'd been pale. Her blue eyes had looked wounded when he'd said, 'I'm sorry.'

He thought of her words: *You've made me see how strong I am.*

Luca felt disgusted. And how strong was *he*? Had he ever gone toe-to-toe with his own demons? No, because he'd told himself building up trust in the Fonseca name again was more important.

He heard a sound and looked up to see a plane lifting into the sky from the airport. He knew it couldn't be her plane, but he had a sudden image of her on it, leaving, and panic gripped him so acutely that he almost called out.

It was as clear as day to him now—what lay between him and his brother. He should have ranted and railed that day when their parents had so cruelly split them up. He should have let it out—not buried it so deep that he'd behaved like a robot since then, afraid to feel anything. Afraid to face the guilt of knowing that he could have done more to protect them both.

If he'd let out the depth of his anger and pain, as Max had, then maybe they wouldn't have been split apart. Two halves of a whole, torn asunder. Maybe their parents would have been forced to acknowledge the shallow depths of their actions, their intent of scoring points off each other.

It all bubbled up now—and also the sick realisation that he was letting it happen all over again. That while he'd had an excuse of sorts before, because he'd only been a child, he was an adult now—and if he couldn't shout and scream for what he wanted then he and Max had been pawns for nothing.

And, worse, he'd face a life devoid of any meaning or any prospect of happiness. Happiness had never concerned him before now. He'd been content to focus on loftier concerns, telling himself it was enough. And it wasn't. Not any more.

Serena stood in line for the gate in the first-class lounge. She was grateful for it, because there was enough space there for her to feel numb and not to have to deal with a crush of people around her.

She couldn't let herself think of Luca, even though her circling thoughts kept coming back to him and that stark look on his face. *I'm sorry.*

She was sorry too. Now she knew how he'd felt when he'd told her that he wished he'd never set eyes on her.

She wanted to feel that way too—she actively encouraged it to come up. But it wouldn't. Because she couldn't regret knowing him. Or loving him. Even if he couldn't love her back.

For a wild moment Serena thought of turning around and going back, telling him she'd settle for whatever he could give her... And then she saw herself in a few years...months...? Her soul shrivelled up from not being loved in return.

The man ahead of her moved forward and the airline steward was reaching for her boarding pass.

She was about to take it back and go through when she heard a sort of commotion, and then a familiar voice shouting, 'I need to see her!'

She whirled around to see Luca being restrained by two staff members a few feet away, dishevelled and wild-looking in shirt and trousers.

'What are you *doing*?' she gasped in shock, stepping out of the way so that people could continue boarding.

She wouldn't let her heart beat fast. She couldn't. It didn't mean anything.

His eyes were fierce. 'Please don't go. I need you to stay.'

A feeling of euphoria mixed with pain surged through her. 'Why do you want me to stay, Luca?'

The men holding him kept a tight grip. Luca didn't even seem to notice, though. He looked feverish, as if he was burning up.

His voice was rough with emotion. 'When you told me you loved me...I couldn't believe it. I was too afraid to believe. My mother said that to me right before she swapped me for my brother...as if we were nothing.'

Serena's belly clenched. 'Oh, Luca...' She looked at the security men, beseeching, 'Please let him go.'

They finally did, but stayed close by, ready to move in again. Serena didn't care. She was oblivious.

He took her hand and held it to his chest, dragging her closer. She could feel his heart thudding against his chest.

'You say you love me…but a part of me can't trust it…can't believe it. I'm terrified that you'll turn around one day and walk away—confirm all my twisted suspicions that when people say they love you, they'll annihilate you anyway.'

Serena felt an incredible welling of love and reached out her other hand to touch Luca's face. She knew he was scared.

'Do you love me?'

After a long moment—long enough for her to see how hard this was for him to admit—he said, 'The thought of you leaving, of life without you…is more than I can bear. If that's love then, yes, I love you more than I've loved anyone else.'

Serena's heart overflowed. 'Are you willing to let me prove how much I love you?'

Luca nodded. 'The pain of letting you go is worse than the pain of facing my own pathetic fears. You've humbled me with your strength and grace.'

She shook her head, tears making her vision blurry. 'They're not pathetic fears, Luca. I'm just as scared as you are.'

He smiled, and it was shaky, all that arrogant bravado replaced by raw emotion. He joked, 'You? Scared? Not possible. You're the bravest person I know. And I have no intention of ever letting you out of my sight again.'

Serena smiled and fought back tears as Luca pulled her in to him and covered her mouth with his, kissing her with unrestrained passion.

When they separated, the crowd around them clapped and cheered. Giddy, Serena blushed and ducked her head against Luca's neck.

He looked at her. 'Will you come home with me?'

Home. Her own place—with him.

The ferocity and speed with which they'd found each other terrified her for a moment. *Could she trust it?* But she saw everything she felt mirrored in Luca's eyes, and she reached out and snatched the dream before it could disappear.

'Yes.'

The next day when Serena woke up she pulled on a big T-shirt and went looking for Luca in his house in Alto Gavea. She still felt a little dizzy from everything that had happened. She and Luca had come back here from the airport, and after making love they'd talked until dawn had broken. He'd promised to go to Athens with her to start the lengthy process of telling her family everything and pursuing her father.

She heard a noise as she passed his study and went in to see him sitting behind his desk in only jeans. Stubbled jaw. He looked up and smiled, and Serena couldn't help smiling back goofily.

He held out a hand. 'Come here.'

She went over and let him catch her, pulling her onto his lap. After some breathless kisses she moved back. 'What are you doing?'

A glint of something came into his eyes and he said, 'Catching up on local news.'

He indicated with his head to the computer and Serena turned to look. When she realised what she was seeing, she tensed in his arms. The internet was filled with photos of them kissing passionately in the airport—obviously taken by people's mobile phones. One headline screamed: *Has Fonseca tamed wild-child DePiero at last*? Another one: *Fonseca and DePiero rekindle their scandalous romance!*

She felt sick and turned to Luca, who was watching her carefully. 'I'm sorry. This is exactly what you were afraid of.'

But he just shrugged, eyes bright and clear. No shadows. 'I couldn't care less what they say. And they have it wrong—you tamed *me*.'

Serena let the past fall away and caressed Luca's jaw, love rising to make her throat tight. 'I love you just as you are.'

Luca said gruffly, 'I want to take you to every beach in South America to watch the sunset—starting with the ones here in Rio.'

Serena felt breathless. 'That could take some time.'

Luca kissed her and said, 'At least a lifetime, I'm hoping.'

He deliberately lifted up her left hand then, and pressed a kiss to her ring finger, a question in his eyes and a new tension in his body. Serena's heart ached that he might still doubt her love.

She nodded her head and said simply, 'Yes. The answer will always be yes, my love.'

Three years later.

The wide-eyed American reporter was standing in front of Rome's supreme court and saying breathlessly, 'This is the trial of the decade—if not the century. Lorenzo DePiero has finally been judged and condemned for his brutality and corruption, but no one could have foreseen the extent to which his own children and his wife suffered. His landmark sentencing will almost certainly guarantee that he lives out the rest of his days in jail.'

The press were still stunned to have discovered that the privileged life they'd assumed the DePiero heiresses to have lived had all been a lie.

Behind the reporter there was a flurry of activity as people streamed out of the majestic building. First was Rocco De Marco, the illegitimate son of Lorenzo De-Piero, with his petite red-haired wife Gracie. Quickly on their heels were Siena Xenakis and her husband An-dreas.

But the press waited with hushed reverence for the person they wanted to see most: Serena Fonseca. She had taken the stand for four long days in a row and had listed a litany of charges against her father. Not least of which had been the manslaughter of his wife, their mother, witnessed by her when she was just five years old.

If anyone had been in doubt about the reliability of a witness who had been only five at the time, the further evidence of her father's systematic bullying and collu-sion with a corrupt doctor to get her hooked on medi-cation had killed those doubts.

Her composed beauty had been all the more poi-gnant for the fact that she hadn't let her very advanced pregnancy stop her from taking on such an arduous task: facing down her father every day. But then, ev-eryone agreed that the constant presence by her side of her husband, Luca Fonseca, had undoubtedly given her strength.

They finally emerged now—a striking couple. Luca Fonseca had an arm curved protectively around his wife and the press captured their visible smiles of relief.

Lawyers for the respective parties gave statements as the family got into their various vehicles and were whisked away with a police escort to a secret location, where they were all due to celebrate and unwind after the previous taxing months.

Luca looked at Serena in the back of the Land Rover, their hands entwined. He lifted them up and pressed a kiss to her knuckles. 'Okay?'

Serena smiled. She felt as if a weight had finally been lifted off her shoulders for the first time in her life. She nodded. 'Tired…but happy it's finally done and over.'

Luca pressed a long, lingering kiss to her mouth, but when he pulled back, Serena frowned and looked down. Immediately concerned, Luca said, 'What is it?'

Serena looked at him, a dawning expression of shock and wonder on her face. 'My waters have just broken… all over the back seat.'

The driver's eyes widened in the rearview mirror and he discreetly took out a mobile phone to make a call.

Serena giggled at the comic look of shock and pure fear on Luca's face. He'd been on high alert for weeks now, overreacting to every twinge Serena felt. And then it hit her—along with a very definite cramping of pain.

Her hand tightened on his. 'Oh, my God, we're in labour.'

Luca went into overdrive, instructing the driver to go to the nearest hospital.

Their police escort was already peeling away from the rest of the convoy and the driver reassured him in Italian, 'I'm on it—we'll be there in ten minutes.'

Luca sat back, heart pumping with adrenalin, a huge ball of love and emotion making his chest full. He drank in his beloved wife, her beautiful face, and those eyes that never failed to suck him in and make him feel as if he were drowning.

'I love you,' he whispered huskily, the words flowing easily from his heart.

'I love you too.'

Serena smiled, but it was wobbly. He could see the emotion in her eyes mirrored his own. He spread his hand over her distended belly, hard with their child who was now starting the journey to meet them.

His wife, his family...*his life*. He was enriched beyond anything he might have believed possible.

And eight hours later, when he held his newborn baby daughter in his arms, her tiny face scrunched up and more beautiful than anything he'd ever seen in his life—after his wife—Luca knew that trusting in love was the most amazing revelation of all.

* * * * *

Mills & Boon® Hardback

January 2015

ROMANCE

The Secret His Mistress Carried	Lynne Graham
Nine Months to Redeem Him	Jennie Lucas
Fonseca's Fury	Abby Green
The Russian's Ultimatum	Michelle Smart
To Sin with the Tycoon	Cathy Williams
The Last Heir of Monterrato	Andie Brock
Inherited by Her Enemy	Sara Craven
Sheikh's Desert Duty	Maisey Yates
The Honeymoon Arrangement	Joss Wood
Who's Calling the Shots?	Jennifer Rae
The Scandal Behind the Wedding	Bella Frances
The Bridegroom Wishlist	Tanya Wright
Taming the French Tycoon	Rebecca Winters
His Very Convenient Bride	Sophie Pembroke
The Heir's Unexpected Return	Jackie Braun
The Prince She Never Forgot	Scarlet Wilson
A Child to Bind Them	Lucy Clark
The Baby That Changed Her Life	Louisa Heaton

MEDICAL

How to Find a Man in Five Dates	Tina Beckett
Breaking Her No-Dating Rule	Amalie Berlin
It Happened One Night Shift	Amy Andrews
Tamed by Her Army Doc's Touch	Lucy Ryder

Mills & Boon® Large Print
January 2015

ROMANCE

The Housekeeper's Awakening — Sharon Kendrick
More Precious than a Crown — Carol Marinelli
Captured by the Sheikh — Kate Hewitt
A Night in the Prince's Bed — Chantelle Shaw
Damaso Claims His Heir — Annie West
Changing Constantinou's Game — Jennifer Hayward
The Ultimate Revenge — Victoria Parker
Interview with a Tycoon — Cara Colter
Her Boss by Arrangement — Teresa Carpenter
In Her Rival's Arms — Alison Roberts
Frozen Heart, Melting Kiss — Ellie Darkins

HISTORICAL

Lord Havelock's List — Annie Burrows
The Gentleman Rogue — Margaret McPhee
Never Trust a Rebel — Sarah Mallory
Saved by the Viking Warrior — Michelle Styles
The Pirate Hunter — Laura Martin

MEDICAL

200 Harley Street: The Shameless Maverick — Louisa George
200 Harley Street: The Tortured Hero — Amy Andrews
A Home for the Hot-Shot Doc — Dianne Drake
A Doctor's Confession — Dianne Drake
The Accidental Daddy — Meredith Webber
Pregnant with the Soldier's Son — Amy Ruttan

1214 GEN STD LP

MILLS & BOON®
Hardback – February 2015

ROMANCE

The Redemption of Darius Sterne	Carole Mortimer
The Sultan's Harem Bride	Annie West
Playing by the Greek's Rules	Sarah Morgan
Innocent in His Diamonds	Maya Blake
To Wear His Ring Again	Chantelle Shaw
The Man to Be Reckoned With	Tara Pammi
Claimed by the Sheikh	Rachael Thomas
Delucca's Marriage Contract	Abby Green
Her Brooding Italian Boss	Susan Meier
The Heiress's Secret Baby	Jessica Gilmore
A Pregnancy, a Party & a Proposal	Teresa Carpenter
Best Friend to Wife and Mother?	Caroline Anderson
The Sheikh Doctor's Bride	Meredith Webber
A Baby to Heal Their Hearts	Kate Hardy
One Hot Desert Night	Kristi Gold
Snowed In with Her Ex	Andrea Laurence
Cowgirls Don't Cry	Silver James
Terms of a Texas Marriage	Lauren Canan

MEDICAL

A Date with Her Valentine Doc	Melanie Milburne
It Happened in Paris...	Robin Gianna
Temptation in Paradise	Joanna Neil
The Surgeon's Baby Secret	Amber McKenzie

MILLS & BOON®
Large Print – February 2015

ROMANCE

An Heiress for His Empire	Lucy Monroe
His for a Price	Caitlin Crews
Commanded by the Sheikh	Kate Hewitt
The Valquez Bride	Melanie Milburne
The Uncompromising Italian	Cathy Williams
Prince Hafiz's Only Vice	Susanna Carr
A Deal Before the Altar	Rachael Thomas
The Billionaire in Disguise	Soraya Lane
The Unexpected Honeymoon	Barbara Wallace
A Princess by Christmas	Jennifer Faye
His Reluctant Cinderella	Jessica Gilmore

HISTORICAL

Zachary Black: Duke of Debauchery	Carole Mortimer
The Truth About Lady Felkirk	Christine Merrill
The Courtesan's Book of Secrets	Georgie Lee
Betrayed by His Kiss	Amanda McCabe
Falling for Her Captor	Elisabeth Hobbes

MEDICAL

Tempted by Her Boss	Scarlet Wilson
His Girl From Nowhere	Tina Beckett
Falling For Dr Dimitriou	Anne Fraser
Return of Dr Irresistible	Amalie Berlin
Daring to Date Her Boss	Joanna Neil
A Doctor to Heal Her Heart	Annie Claydon